WEARING THE ITALIAN SURGEON'S RING

JC HARROWAY

Recycling programs for this product may not exist in your area.

ISBN-13: 978-1-335-99378-6

Wearing the Italian Surgeon's Ring

For questions and comments about the quality of this book, please contact us at CustomerService@Harlequin.com.

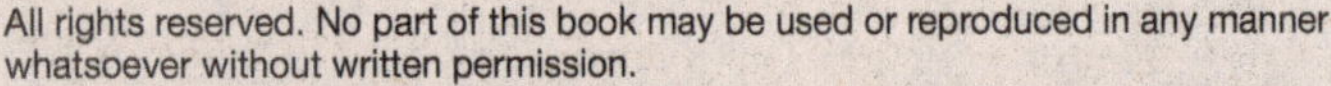

Harlequin Enterprises ULC
22 Adelaide St. West, 41st Floor
Toronto, Ontario M5H 4E3, Canada
www.Harlequin.com

HarperCollins Publishers
Macken House, 39/40 Mayor Street Upper,
Dublin 1, D01 C9W8, Ireland
www.HarperCollins.com

Printed in U.S.A.

1 2 3 4 5 6 7 8 9 10 HDC 28 27 26 25

Mediterranean Docs

A summer of medicine and romance!

It's not all sun, sea and fun in the Mediterranean...
It's pulse-racing emergencies, ER drama
and a few medical miracles, too.
As these medics know all too well!

But while they're working hard, there's no doubt they're playing hard... So, grab a one-way ticket to Europe to see what they're getting up to in their downtime. Rest assured that things are heating up!

Discover more in

Greek Hospital, Red-Hot Reunion
by Tina Beckett

Wearing the Italian Surgeon's Ring
by JC Harroway

Available now!

How to Date a Doc in Barcelona
by Juliette Hyland

Surgeon's Plus-One in Provence
by Tessa Scott

Coming next month!

Dear Reader,

In writing a story for Mediterranean Month, it was easy to capture the history, tradition and passion of the region in Marco and Elena's tale.

I was lucky enough to visit Capri at age sixteen, and, as most people do, I imagine, I fell instantly in love. Not only with the glamour and beauty of the place itself, but also with a handsome crew member on the ferry called Mimo, who taught me the phrase "Ciao bella." We might have met for only five minutes, and I'm sure I wasn't the only tourist he flirted with that summer, but the magic of that moment and of Capri itself have always stayed with me.

I hope that in reading *Wearing the Italian Surgeon's Ring*, you, too, fall in love with Capri.

Love,

JC x

Lifelong romance addict **JC Harroway** took a break from her career as a junior doctor to raise a family and found her calling as a Harlequin author instead. She now lives in New Zealand and finds that writing feeds her very real obsession with happy endings and the endorphin rush they create. You can follow her at jcharroway.com and on Facebook, X and Instagram.

Books by JC Harroway

Harlequin Medical Romance

Buenos Aires Docs

Secretly Dating the Baby Doc

Jet Set Docs

One Night to Sydney Wedding

Royally Tempted

One Night to Royal Baby

Sexy Surgeons in the City

Manhattan Marriage Reunion

Nurse's Secret Royal Fling
Forbidden Fiji Nights with Her Rival
The Midwife's Secret Fling
Mistletoe Baby Mix-Up
The Paramedic Roommate Pact
Doctor Boss with Benefits

Visit the Author Profile page
at Harlequin.com for more titles.

To my sixteen-year-old self,
already a die-hard romantic. Keep believing in love.

CHAPTER ONE

Surgical oncologist Dr Marco Caruso left the sun-baked heat of another perfect Mediterranean day and stepped inside the cool air-conditioned interior of Capri's Santa Maria Clinic. At his office, a south-facing room on the third floor with incredible views of the island and the Tyrrhenian Sea beyond towards Sorrento, he donned his suit jacket, catching sight of a message from his secretary on the desk:

Please call Signore Papini at Papini, Vicario and Borla Law.

With one eye on the time, Marco swiftly dialled the number he'd learned by heart since his grandfather had passed and was immediately put through to Nonno's probate lawyer, based in nearby Naples.

'Dr Caruso,' the man said. 'Thank you for returning my call so promptly.'

'I'm on my way to a surgery,' Marco said, pausing for Papini to get straight to the point. His mind was on the long day ahead and the complex Whipple surgery on one of Italy's most prominent former political figures, Fredo Degano.

'I won't keep you,' Papini said. 'I've also emailed the information through, but wanted to be sure you understood the condition eight-point-two-A in your grandfather's will.'

Again, Marco waited.

'As I'm sure you are aware, the Caruso estate is ancient,' the lawyer continued, 'and, I'm afraid, so are its laws of inheritance. The property should, of course, have gone to your late father, but, as his only son, now passes to you.'

'Yes, I'm aware of that.' Marco bit back a sigh as the dull ache of grief gnawed at his chest. He'd grown up knowing the estate would one day be his, after his beloved father, Dario. It was something Marco had almost taken for granted. Of course, he couldn't have known that Nonno would outlive his son, Marco's father. Couldn't have predicted Dario Caruso's untimely and unexpected death. But Marco *would* finish the dream he and his father had planned for the estate.

'Yes, well, unfortunately, clause eight-point-two-A, the legacy clause, states that the estate in its entirety must stay within the Caruso family.'

'I am a Caruso,' Marco pointed out, his patience fraying.

'Yes,' Papini said with a nervous throat-clearing. 'But it also states that the legacy, the estate, must be protected for future generations of Carusos. So I'm afraid that, in order to inherit, you must be married or have fathered an heir and... Well, neither of those stipulations apply.'

Marco froze, his heart thudding in his chest.

'That's preposterous and antiquated,' he said, his analytical surgeon's mind rebelling against the illogical. What difference did his marital status make? He'd been married once before and that hadn't lasted long or resulted in a family. He'd always imagined he might remarry at some point in the future, but his contentious divorce from Bianca had left him in no particular hurry, given she'd almost broken up the estate with her unreasonable divorce demands.

'Quite,' the lawyer agreed, sounding rather smug. 'But I'm afraid there is no way around it. Obviously, if the estate had first passed to your father before you, then there might have been no need for this conversation down the track. You might, by then, have remarried.'

Marco's thoughts raced, his fingers curled into a fist as renewed guilt all but choked him. The Caruso estate had been in his family for hundreds of years. Nestled in the greenery of its own private park, the estate consisted of five villas, the largest boasting fifteen bedrooms, a pool, a guest house and guardian's accommodation. Ample room for separate residences for Marco, his mother and sister, and for the small, specialist hospital he and his father had dreamed of one day opening.

Marco fully intended to complete the Caruso Cancer Centre, named in honour of his father. He'd promised Dario in his last days that he *would* build it. And after his father had helped him to pay off his ex-wife, Marco owed him and would not let him down.

'And if I do not meet this condition of the will?' he asked, the contempt he felt for such an absurd stipulation obvious in his voice. He wasn't even seeing anyone at the moment.

'Then the estate in its entirety will be donated to charity, I'm afraid.'

Marco clenched his jaw as pressure built in his head. He had responsibilities. Not just to his and Dario's dream, but also to his widowed mother and younger sister, Ginevra, who, like him, considered the Caruso estate home. His mother had lost the love of her life to stomach cancer last year and Gin had been forced to step in and take over the running of their father's business interests, Caruso Enterprises. They couldn't lose their Capri sanctuary on top of everything else.

Another glance at the wall clock enabled him to bat away the inconvenient news. 'I'll need to call you back this afternoon, Signore Papini,' Marco said, ending the call. He strode from his office and took the stairs down to the pre-op surgical ward, his thoughts turning to his patient and the lengthy surgery ahead. He would find a solution to the unforeseen problem. He always did.

On the ward, he paused at the receptionist's desk. '*Buongiorno,* Luisa. Has Dr Renzi arrived yet to see Signore Degano?' he asked about his registrar.

The receptionist looked taken aback. 'Haven't

you heard? Dr Renzi broke his femur hang-gliding at the weekend. He was flown to the orthopaedic hospital in Naples.'

Marco pressed his lips together, holding in his second sigh of the morning. It wasn't even eight a.m. 'Is there any word on his condition?' he asked of Renzi, an experienced surgeon who knew their high-profile patient almost as well as Marco himself.

'I understand he's awaiting surgery,' Luisa said, 'but is stable, apart from the broken bone.'

'Very good.' Marco reached for one of the ward tablets from the docking station, already contingency planning around the inconvenience. He would see if one of the other registrars was free to assist him in Theatre today. The Whipple procedure was complex and time-consuming and required two surgeons.

'But don't worry, Dr Caruso,' Luisa called after him. 'The locum is already with the patient.'

'Locum?' Marco's stomach sank. That last thing he needed today of all days was an incxperienced surgeon to babysit. One who knew nothing of the case or the patient and nothing of Marco's high expectations for his work.

Cancer often had the upper hand by the time it presented, but with meticulous staging and surgery they could, for the majority of patients, even up the odds.

'Yes. She's with him now,' Luisa said, her smile

fading at Marco's frown. 'She's been here since seven. She's on Dr Brienza's team but said she wanted to get to know today's pre-op patients.'

Biting his tongue, Marco nodded and headed for Degano's room, pulling out his phone to message Dr Brienza, one of his consultant colleagues. He always told the registrars he trained that one of the most important personality traits for a surgeon was adaptability. Until you opened the patient up, you never truly knew exactly what you would find. Thinking and acting on the fly was a crucial skill, and one he would employ now in the face of this morning's unforeseen complications. And with Dr Renzi out of action, this locum would need to divide their time between Marco and his consultant colleague until another could be appointed.

Having hastily sent a message to Dr Brienza, explaining Dr Renzi's accident and arranging to borrow her locum registrar for the Whipple procedure today, Marco briefly tapped on the closed door of his patient. Wondering what he would find in the young surgeon the universe had sent him, he entered the room.

Elena Mancini perched on the edge of the bed belonging to Fredo Degano, the retired politician she'd long admired from afar and her newest patient.

'And does your grandson play for a team?' she asked Degano, while also taking his pulse, noting it was strong and regular, if slightly elevated. The man was trying to stay positive, but was clearly nervous for his major operation today.

The patient returned her smile with pride. 'He plays for his school team but he wants to play for Azzurri, of course.'

'What eleven-year-old football fan doesn't want to represent Italy on the field?' Elena said, standing and opening the back of the man's hospital gown to listen to his breathing.

With her auscultation complete, she removed her stethoscope. 'Well, everything seems good for your surgery today,' she said, looping the stethoscope around her neck. 'I believe the consultant will see you before the operation. Do you have any questions for me in the meantime?'

Degano shook his head. 'Thank you, Dr Mancini. It was lovely to meet a fellow Napoletano. You are a ray of sunshine.'

'It was lovely to meet you too.' Elena laughed, glad to have momentarily taken this lovely man's mind off his surgery. 'I've always admired you. I even voted for you a few times,' she said in a stage whisper and then laughed.

But her distraction technique also cloaked the relief she felt that this man hadn't recognised *her* name. Or, if he did know of her family's past legal woes and bankruptcy scandal, he was kind and respectful enough not to mention it. Sadly, not everyone she met was as accepting of Gio Mancini's daughter as Signore Degano.

'I'll see you in Theatre, before they put you to sleep,' she said. 'And then again when you wake up and it's all over, okay?'

Elena was just about to step away from the end of the man's bed when a short tap at the door sounded. She looked up as a tall man in an immaculate navy suit strode into the room, immediately commanding the space with his air of authority. And something about him struck Elena as vaguely familiar.

Handsome and confident, he stood at well over six feet tall. His broad shoulders and well-defined chest and arms filled the suit and crisp white shirt in a way indicative of time spent at the gym. His dark brown hair and closely trimmed beard showed only the lightest smattering of grey, so she would put him in his forties. But it was the expression in his coffee-coloured eyes that gave away his superior status. Coolly assessing, they briefly, almost dismissively, swept over Elena before landing on Degano.

'Signore Degano,' the newcomer said, shaking the other man's hand. 'Are you ready for today?'

Elena stood her ground at the foot of the bed, refusing to scuttle away with her head down. She'd spent enough time diminished by shame after her family's professional and financial misfortune. After recovering from her broken heart when her ex, Rocco, had betrayed Elena and her family over the scandal, she'd vowed never again to hang her head. Her father was a good man, a good surgeon, who'd made one mistake. But hadn't he since paid enough of a price, both financially and with his poor health?

Elena observed the senior surgeon, assuming he was one of the consultants at SMC. Weeks ago, when she'd applied for a locum position here, she'd learned she was to work for Dr Brienza, a female surgical oncologist whose usual registrar was on maternity leave. This man was most definitely not Dr Brienza.

'Raring to go,' the patient replied, the slightest wobble of nervousness back in his expression.

Elena offered the patient another encouraging smile. Who wouldn't be nervous? His surgery would be long and challenging and only the start of his treatment journey. He faced a gruelling post-op recovery and possible chemotherapy, depending on the pathology results.

'Good,' the consultant said, without offering a single word of comfort. 'Nothing has changed since your last outpatient appointment, where we discussed everything in full detail. The surgery we planned together will go ahead today. But as I explained to you, things might change once I have a scalpel in my hand. The scans can only tell us so much. I need to see the extent of your disease with my own eyes.'

Signore Degano nodded, his face pale. 'Thank you, Dr Caruso. I put myself in your excellent hands.'

As the patient's words of faith registered, Elena's

blood froze. Dr Caruso? Not Marco Caruso, son of Dario Caruso, her father's former friend, surgical colleague and business partner?

Her mouth dried. She'd never met his son, but she'd heard Dario Caruso's name so many times over the years, her body instantly reacted—her hackles rising, her temperature soaring, her stare scouring the man who shared his name for any sign of recognition.

'Then let us begin,' Caruso said rather stiffly, turning for the door.

Elena hesitated, stunned by Caruso's coolness and rather abrupt, no-frills bedside manner. In addition, he'd barely glanced her way and was yet to address her personally. What an insufferably arrogant man… But if he was the Caruso she suspected, could she truly expect anything more? His father too was ruthless, using her own dear papà's relative inexperience for business to ensure that he emerged unscathed from the scandal that had closed their joint plastic surgery clinic in Naples, Medicina dell'Apparenza. And worse, Dario had publicly turned on Gio Mancini in the end, choosing to make a public statement and protect his own reputation as a surgeon over loyalty to their friendship and surgical partnership.

At the door, Caruso paused, his aloof gaze sweeping over Elena once more. 'Doctor, a word outside, please.'

Elena followed him into the plushly carpeted

corridor, pausing only to give the patient one final reassuring smile, even though her own stomach churned. Outside the patient's room and up close, she had to tilt her chin to look up at Caruso. But at least it would give him the correct impression: that she was not intimidated by him.

'I'm assuming you are the locum registrar?' he asked without the smallest attempt to appear welcoming or even polite.

Because he already knew her name? Was he unfairly judging her before they'd even met, just because she was a Mancini? Working in the same field as her father, she'd faced similar prejudice before, but refused to be ashamed of who she was or of her kind and intelligent papà.

'I am a locum. But I understood I was working for Dr Brienza. Just like I was told to perform a pre-op examination of Signore Degano when I arrived on the ward this morning.'

'You are to work for me, too,' he said with a frown, heading for the stairwell, obviously assuming she would meekly follow.

She did, but only because she didn't want this man to have the last word.

'No one told me that,' she said, rushing to keep pace with his long-legged stride as he descended the stairs.

If he was Dario Caruso's son, he was the last man on earth for whom she'd ever voluntarily work. When a patient had sued Gio Mancini and Medicina dell'Apparenza for medical misadventure after disappointing surgical results, this man's father had saved his own skin rather than stand united with hers. And while Caruso Enterprises and the Caruso family had emerged from the scandal and aborted partnership financially healthy, *her* beloved father, her family, had lost nearly everything: most of Mancini Holdings' business interests, her father's professional reputation as a surgeon, even his health. She hated Marco Caruso for his surname alone, regardless of how disarmingly attractive he was.

'Might I know why?' she asked as they passed through another door and Caruso scanned his security tag to unlock a restricted access to theatres.

'My registrar has a penchant for extreme sports,' he said unemotionally. 'He fractured his femur in a hang-gliding accident over the weekend.'

He paused outside the theatre changing rooms, casting her a look of impatience. If he didn't yet know who she was, if he simply considered her a locum not up to his standards, he was insufferably rude.

Elena hadn't realised she'd sighed aloud until he nodded, his frown deepening, and said, 'Quite. I agree. This…situation is not ideal for either of us, or for the patient. This surgery has been meticulously planned for weeks. My registrar knew the case and the patient inside out. Whereas you…'

Elena gaped, her face heating at his unfair and

unfounded assessment. 'What is that supposed to mean? You don't even know me. Yet you have already made up your mind that I am incapable of doing my job.'

Now *she* was being rude, addressing a consultant that way, something she would never normally do. But ever since the litigation scandal involving her father, ever since the story had been splashed all over the news, she'd learned that some unfairly judged her by association and to toughen up.

'I might be a locum,' she continued defensively, 'but I assure you that my references are glowing. I have over a hundred hours of operating time under my belt, and I am more than capable of assisting you in place of your registrar. I came in early this morning to meet the pre-op patients and have read all of Signore Degano's notes and studied the scans and biopsy results.'

As if he'd only just spied it, Caruso stared at the name tag she'd clipped to the waistband of her scrub trousers that morning, his cool expression chilling further and his stare darkening to almost black as his eyes re-met hers. 'Elena Mancini. Is that your name?'

She tilted her chin in defiance. So he hadn't known who she was before, but was about to. He *was* simply rude and unwelcoming to locums.

'Are you related to Gio Mancini?' A muscle twitched in his jaw as he pinned her with a glare that left her in no doubt that her worst fear was correct. This man was the enemy: Dario Caruso's son. And the bad blood between their families was very much still flowing.

'That's right. I'm his daughter.' She returned his stare, unblinking. 'And I assume that you are *Marco* Caruso?' Why else would he be looking at her with such obvious contempt? The exact same emotion she felt for him, given their families' history.

'Indeed,' he said, his stare glittering with instant dislike, even as his mouth curved into an insincere smile. 'Welcome to SMC, Dr Mancini. I operate in Theatre Three. I'll see you inside.'

Dismissing her, he turned and entered the male changing rooms, the door swinging closed behind him, leaving Elena to stare after him, dumbfounded. She tried to catch her ragged breath, feeling as if she'd been picked up and deposited by a tornado.

But if Marco Caruso expected her to slink away, ashamed of her name, her father, his mistake, he'd misjudged her and her family. Gio Mancini had operated on the patient who'd gone on to sue him and Medicina dell'Apparenza with full consent and to the best of his ability. His only error had been trying to defend his name and that of the clinic in court rather than settle. He wasn't a bad man. Just a human being. Elena was proud to be his daughter and to follow in his footsteps as a surgeon.

Swallowing the acidic taste that came when she

considered that, by working for Marco Caruso, she was betraying her beloved father when he was currently at his weakest, she flounced down the corridor in search of his operating room. She would show him…

CHAPTER TWO

THE WHIPPLE PROCEDURE, or pancreaticoduodenectomy, was one of the most challenging operations a surgical oncologist performed. Marco always blocked out the entire day for this type of case. The surgery, which often lasted up to eight hours in duration, required all of his concentration, which was why the minute he'd changed out of his suit and donned his SMC scrubs he'd shoved all thoughts of Elena Mancini, her dark accusing eyes, fiery spirit and stunning beauty from his mind.

She was not her father, of course. But she was an unknown. Marco partly blamed Gio Mancini—his refusal to settle the case that had ruined the partnership out of court—for his father's diagnosis and death. Stress weakened the immune system, suppressing cells crucial for identifying and destroying early cancer cells. Without the trauma of a public scandal, civil court case and the closure of his Naples clinic, Dario's life in that final year might have been very different.

Signore Degano's operation had, so far, gone as planned. With Elena's assistance, Marco had removed the head of the pancreas where the cancer was located, the gallbladder, the distal part of the stomach and the duodenum. With the surgical specimen on its way to the pathology lab, Marco set about re-fashioning the remaining parts back together to rebuild the patient's upper digestive tract.

But as he carefully sutured what was left of the pancreatic duct into the opening he'd created in the small intestine, he took a moment to quiz his locum's surgical knowledge. If she was to work for him, he would not tolerate any slacking. He took pride in his patient outcome statistics because they mattered. As a doctor, he'd always seen the patient and not just the disease. Around every patient there was a network of loved ones. His job was to do everything in his power to give the patient and their family more time together.

'As you've reviewed my patient, Dr Mancini,' he began, glancing at her hazel eyes above her mask, 'and as you have now witnessed the extent of his tumour from our exploration and the surgical resection specimen, tell me what you think Signore Degano's prognosis might be.'

She met his stare, hers bold and challenging, as it had been from the moment she'd followed him from the patient's room earlier. It was obvious she did not like him. But for Marco, that was neither here nor there. Especially not within the hospital walls.

'Assuming the cancer is localized to the pancreas and hasn't spread to the lymph nodes,' she began confidently, 'around forty-four percent of people survive for five years or more.'

Marco nodded for her to continue, precision focused on his sutures.

'If, however, the tumour has spread to the regional lymph nodes,' she continued, 'that's stage IIB and the rate of five-year survival drops to around only fifteen percent.'

'Very good,' Marco said, grudgingly impressed.

As she'd promised, this woman had indeed been capable and helpful throughout the long hours of the operation. That didn't mean he could forget to whom she was related. It had been obvious from the hostile looks she'd shot him earlier that she had known his identity as Dario Caruso's son. Nor did it mean she wouldn't need to prove herself to him, like every other surgical registrar.

'And are you happy that I have removed all of the visible tumour?' he pushed. He always encouraged registrars in training to put themselves in a consultant's shoes and imagine they were operating alone. Because, soon enough, they would be responsible for their own patients.

She nodded, clearly taken aback by his question as if she considered him too arrogant to be humble. 'The pancreatic resection margins were clear of tumour on the frozen sections,' she said. 'So yes. I think you can be confident that you have removed all of the tumour.'

'Confidence is a thorny trait for a surgeon,' he pointed out, looking away from her emotive stare. 'We need to have enough of it in order to open up another human being and get the job done without causing harm, but too much can lead to intolerable mistakes.'

A balance Marco had strived for his entire career, but especially since losing his father. Marco didn't blame Dario's medical team for his death, but nor had it been easy for him to adopt the role of a relative and not the surgeon in charge.

Elena stared wordlessly, sparks of fire in her eyes. Either she disliked his line of questioning or she had a real problem working for him. Either way, she could vote with her feet and locum elsewhere, something he would suggest if the need arose.

Moving on to join the common hepatic duct to a second opening in the small intestine, now that the gallbladder had been removed, Marco continued his questioning. 'And what are the main complications of the surgery we have performed today? What will we be watching for in the days and weeks ahead?'

'Up to one third of patients undergoing a Whipple procedure will develop complications,' she said, her challenging stare unfaltering. 'The main ones include diabetes, post-operative bleeding, wound infection, bile leakage, pancreatic enzyme leaks, fistula formation and delayed gastric emptying.

Longer-term complications include malabsorption and anastomotic strictures.'

'And what further treatment might the patient require once he has recovered from his surgery?' Marco asked a while later, as he began to suture a loop of small intestine to the opening in the stomach to reconnect the alimentary tract and allow for as close to normal digestion as possible.

'Adjuvant chemotherapy has been shown to improve survival, especially in cases of lymph node involvement,' she went on. 'Next steps will depend on the pathology results, the true microscopic extent of the tumour, nodal metastases and resection margins.'

'Indeed. Let's finish up here,' Marco said, casting another critical eye over his work.

Having meticulously re-checked every surgical join and sited drains nearby to monitor for any post-operative leaks of bile or pancreatic enzymes, Marco began to close the abdominal wound.

'I'm happy to close up for you if you'd like,' Elena said, releasing her hold on the retractor she'd held onto for much of the surgery while she'd assisted.

She flexed her fingers as if against stiffness and a flicker of compassion passed through him as he glanced at the operating room clock to see the surgery had entered its ninth hour.

'I close myself,' Marco said, uncaring that many consultants left the job of suturing the patient closed after an operation to the registrar. He looked up and met her stare. 'If you want to touch a scalpel in my OR, Dr Mancini, I'm afraid you'll have to prove yourself worthy.'

He didn't achieve his patient survival rates by chance. He planned, performed and double-checked to the very best of his ability. Because behind every surgery was a human being, their family and loved ones. And Marco now understood first-hand the devastation of losing a relative to cancer. Despite being a surgical oncologist, he hadn't been able to help or save his father. And Dario had done so much for him, especially during Marco's divorce…

The Caruso Cancer Centre would go some small distance to appeasing Marco's guilt and honouring the vibrant, successful family man Dario Caruso had once been. But his dreams would be impossible to achieve unless he could find a way around the frustrating legal stipulations in Nonno's will.

'Very well,' she said and he looked up to see her lovely eyes narrowed with determination. 'I will.'

If he hadn't spent the past nine hours facing her across the operating table, he might have missed her tell-tale flash of annoyance and suspicion. But it was easily ignored. The operation wasn't complete until the patient came out of the anaesthetic. Any personal grudge she possessed would need to be shelved until they were off the clock. And he could match her every reason to dislike and distrust him because of his family name.

When the surgery was over, he removed his gloves and mask. 'I expect hourly reviews of Signore Degano's progress,' he told Elena.

'Of course,' she said stiffly as if his demand was unreasonable. 'I would do this for any patient.' She removed her mask. 'I'll remind you I'm not a medical student, Dr Caruso.'

'I'm glad to hear it,' he said, watching her closely as she pressed her full lips together. She clearly wanted to say more.

'In fact,' she added, proving him right, 'like you, I am from a medical family. Rest assured your patients are in good hands.'

Her implication was thinly veiled. They were no longer ignorant of the other's identity. They obviously each had a view on the unfortunate conclusion of their fathers' former connection, but they did not need to like each other in order to do their jobs.

'Carry on, then,' Marco said.

He de-robed and left Theatre, headed for the changing rooms where he dressed in his own clothes, calmly formulating a plan to deal with the disarmingly beautiful Elena Mancini. His patients always came first and nothing would change that.

But now that he'd met Gio Mancini's daughter and the wounds of their families' pasts had been ripped open, the urgency to honour *his* father became even more pressing, propelling him to succeed at any cost. Restless with impatience, he returned to his office to call his personal lawyer to see what might be done to circumvent his grandfather's stifling will.

Later that night, after answering an urgent call for one of Dr Brienza's patients on the post-op ward, Elena made her way to the High Dependency Unit to check on Signore Degano after his surgery. Her feet throbbed with fatigue after standing in Theatre all day. It was dark outside, and she was desperate for a soak in the bath and her bed. Not, she suspected, that sleep would come easily. She was wound too tight. The fiery part of her nature eager to confront the insufferable Marco Caruso for his growing list of transgressions.

How dared he act so suspicious of her and professionally cold? She wasn't some charlatan with a fake medical degree downloaded off the internet. Until her father's decline from Parkinson's disease only a year after his company's bankruptcy, she'd been solely focused on her surgical career. But with the shock of the diagnosis and no money to pay for external help, Elena had made the choice to temporarily pause her surgical training and assist her mother and brother in tending to her father.

It was only now that Papà required end-of-life care and had been admitted to the Dignità Hospice in Naples that Elena could focus once more on her career. And a locum position allowed her to continue the work she loved while also giving her time to visit her beloved father at the weekends.

She'd just rounded the corner when the door to HDU swung open and Marco appeared. She stalled, frowning that he was still at the hospital at nine o'clock at night when most consultants would have been long gone. He'd donned his suit after the surgery. His shirt was open at the neck, revealing a triangle of bronzed chest and a smattering of dark manly hair that frustratingly drew her attention. The silk tie with which he'd begun their long day was now tucked into his jacket pocket, making him seem more approachable somehow. More human. If that was even possible.

Elena swallowed down the surge of attraction. There was no denying he was a very handsome and virile man. But his arrogance and apparent ruthlessness allowed her to distrust him without a single drop of guilt. And the frown he bestowed on her quickly killed the stirring of heat in her belly.

'Dr Mancini,' he said, the stubble on his face a little darker than it had been that morning, giving him a dangerous brooding quality she had no care for. 'Are you here to see Degano?'

He seemed surprised. No doubt his suspicions extended to her dedication.

'Yes. I've done the hourly post-op reviews you requested,' Elena said, standing tall, wishing she could return his earlier dismissal of her, 'but I thought I'd check on him one last time before I head home.' She always carried out her work to the best of her ability. She refused to allow Marco's attitude to intimidate her, and she'd been unfairly judged before.

Because of the court case and the bankruptcy, her father had lost his professional reputation. People believed the headlines. Believed that if there was a complaint it must have been the surgeon at fault, when the reality was far more nuanced. Appearance medicine was unique in that the surgery was, for the majority of cases, a cosmetic choice. Sometimes, no matter how well-informed of the risks and lack of guarantees, a patient might be dissatisfied with the surgical results. She'd had to become well-practised in working harder than her counterparts in order to prove herself and her name, as unfair as that felt.

Marco gave a curt nod, his stare blank. 'I've just reviewed him myself so there is no need.'

Elena raised her chin defensively. Having experienced first-hand people's unfounded judgement, she usually tried to give others the benefit of the doubt. But after his comments about her ability and proving herself, it seemed that Marco Caruso was determined to test her resolve.

'And how is he doing?' she asked.

Her concern was more personal than a professional box to be ticked. She'd liked Fredo Degano before she'd met him that morning. He was a respected public figure in Italy thanks to his charity work following his retirement from politics. During her brief pre-op examination, she'd learned he was devoted to his growing family, his grandchildren in particular, and had a dry sense of humour he'd clearly kept largely hidden from the public during his career.

'He's asleep,' Caruso said. 'Blood pressure and urine output good. Afebrile and no evidence of anastomotic leakage for now.'

Elena nodded, eager to check the patient for herself as soon as she could bypass her robotic gatekeeper, who seemed only interested in the patient's clinical signs of recovery. 'Has anyone called his wife?'

Marco's stare narrowed. Perhaps he'd picked up on the accusation in her voice. He might be a meticulous surgeon, precise and painstaking, but in her opinion his people skills left something to be desired.

'Of course,' he said, tilting his head as he regarded her. 'I called Signora Degano myself the moment the surgery was complete.'

Elena caught a hint of his enticing cologne and swallowed. That he smelled good was also irrelevant.

'Then I'll let you get home, Dr Caruso.' She stepped around him and reached for her security pass to unlock the doors to HDU, only to pause at his next question.

'Are we going to have a problem working together, you and I?' he asked, his voice low but firm.

Elena turned to face him once more, her chin rising another defiant notch as all the humiliation of the day and the past finally snapped her professional restraint. 'Do you mean because of the history between our fathers? How yours crushed mine, both his reputation *and* his spirit, by that public statement he made, essentially denouncing my father's risk-taking surgical approach. How, as a family, we almost lost everything from the scandal, whereas thanks to Caruso Enterprises' clever business wrangling, your family walked away virtually unscathed.'

If she hadn't been so fatigued, hadn't felt so unfairly judged, she might not have crossed the line so spectacularly. But his dismissive words and veiled put-downs were imprinted on her mind.

'Whereas you... Confidence is a thorny trait for a surgeon...can lead to intolerable mistakes... If you want to touch a scalpel in my OR, Dr Mancini, I'm afraid you'll have to prove yourself worthy.'

'Unscathed?' he said quietly. Fury flashed in his dark eyes like a bolt of lightning. He stepped half a pace closer so Elena was forced to look up at him to maintain eye contact. The heat from his body bathed her like a roaring fire so her chest grew tighter with every breath.

'Rest assured that I'm a professional, Dr Caruso,' she said, ignoring his question and the implication that the Caruso family had also suffered, perhaps from embarrassment. 'I can set aside any personal feelings I have in order to work for you, to do my job to the best of my abilities, as I always do. Despite what you said earlier about mistakes, my father was a good surgeon and I also intend to be one.'

Marco frowned with confusion. 'I was not referring to Gio Mancini when I spoke earlier. But I'm glad to hear you can stay focused while you work here.' His sceptical stare shifted over her face. 'My patients come first within these walls, Dr Mancini. And whatever fairytale you have concocted to explain the fiasco that took down Medicina dell'Apparenza is completely irrelevant.'

'*Fairytale?*' she scoffed, her head buzzing as if her blood pressure had shot up. '*Fiasco?*' He'd done it now. Provoked her fiery temper. Yes, he was her boss, but his coldness, his arrogance, his constant reminders that she'd need to prove herself had finally got to her. So what if he fired her? She'd already survived worse.

'More like nightmare,' she said. 'Mancini Holdings had to file for bankruptcy after the civil ruling. My parents lost their beloved home where they'd raised their family. My father lost his professional reputation *and* his health. He never again worked as a surgeon.'

Elena dragged in a painful breath. The entire Mancini family had lost something, Elena included. She'd lost the man she'd loved, the man she'd assumed she would one day marry and spend her life with. Rocco's betrayal had come when she'd needed him most and made a horrible situation even worse.

Marco's frown deepened, his jaw clenched mulishly, incensing Elena further. But at least her anger and dislike distracted her from the pain and humiliation of her ex's disloyalty.

'Yes,' he said coldly, 'well, sadly, there are greater losses in this world.'

What did that mean? Was he talking about their work, their patients? The damage that cancer could ravage on a person and their loved ones?

But now that she'd crossed a line with her boss, she couldn't seem to stop. 'Your father didn't have to turn on mine so publicly. That statement he made essentially denounced my father's choice of surgery. The very least Caruso Enterprises could do,' she said, taking the opportunity to point out how his family might go some way to making amends, 'is agree to sell their half of Dignità Hospice to the Mancini Foundation run by my brother. But Dino tells me his repeated requests to purchase the Caruso share have gone unanswered for over a year.'

The Mancinis' stake in the hospice was not only the one asset of the Caruso-Mancini partnership to have survived the bankruptcy, the place was also her father's home since his Parkinson's had deteriorated. Bringing the investment under the foundation's umbrella would bring them all peace of mind, especially Papà, who deeply regretted that, because of the bankruptcy, he could not leave his loved ones more security after he died.

'I think we should focus on *our* business,' Marco suggested, ignoring her references. 'The business of surgery and our patients. It is late. I will assume your outburst is down to fatigue. Go home, Dr Mancini.'

And with that final order he strode away, leaving her watching his retreat, certain she had never disliked anyone more and equally certain that her locum position at SMC might have come to a premature end.

CHAPTER THREE

THE NEXT MORNING, after a restless night where he not only replayed his every infuriating interaction with Elena Mancini but also ruminated on the issue of his inheritance, Marco arrived at SMC before eight a.m. and headed straight for HDU and Signore Degano. His lawyer had assured him that the legacy clause could not be challenged or circumvented, leaving Marco only one option: to find a wife and fast.

He'd vowed after his divorce from Bianca that he would not rush into another long-term relationship. He certainly would not choose to rush into marriage again. But, unlike his first marriage, this second necessary one needn't be the real thing or have anything to do with feelings. He just needed to find the right woman…

As he walked onto HDU, grateful to have a distraction from the claustrophobic idea of finding a wife after the havoc Bianca had wreaked, he glanced over at Signore Degano's bed.

To his frustration, Elena was already with the patient. It was as if she was intent on showing him her dedication. Was there no escaping the woman?

He watched her for a moment, once again witness to her open smile and effortless engaging manner. Signore Degano looked at her as if he'd awoken from his anaesthetic to find an angel at his bedside.

Marco stiffened, irrationally unsettled that his registrar seemed to bestow that smile on everyone *but* him. Given their lack of trust and the accusations she'd hurled the day before, it was only to be expected. But what left him conflicted was just how much it bothered him.

'Dr Mancini,' Marco said as he arrived at the bedside, noticing escaped wisps of her hair brush her elegant neck beneath her ponytail.

As predicted, Elena instantly dropped her smile and hardened her expression, and he brushed aside another prickle of frustration. 'Signore Degano, *buongiorno*,' he said. 'Excuse us a moment while Dr Mancini tells me how you're doing this morning.'

From across the bed, Marco gave Elena a nod and reached for the patient's observation chart. He scanned the overnight recordings of pulse, blood pressure, temperature and urine output while she spoke.

'As you can see from the chart,' she said, 'Signore Degano has developed a low-grade fever overnight. The amylase level in the pancreatic drain this morning is moderate, which, if it remains high in the coming days, might prove suggestive of the formation of pancreatic fistula.'

Marco shrugged, hoping for the best for the sake of their patient. A leak of pancreatic enzymes following a Whipple procedure was common. The gland was soft and fragile. 'Keep measuring the levels,' he suggested. 'They may fall as the days pass.'

Elena nodded and continued. 'I've examined Signore Degano this morning and there's no evidence of consolidation in the chest and the wound looks good.'

'Run the usual post-operative blood tests plus a blood culture,' Marco instructed, ignoring the way her pretty eyes returned to the patient often, along with her lovely encouraging smile. 'We will watch the fever today and if it doesn't settle, we might consider a scan or switching antibiotics.'

He turned to the patient's nurse, who had joined them at the bedside. 'Has the dietitian referral been made?'

'Yes, Dr Caruso. She will be on the ward later this morning.'

Marco nodded. 'Ask the physiotherapist to get him moving. We don't want him developing a deep vein thrombosis.'

The nurse made a note and Marco turned to address the patient once more. 'Your tests and observations are mostly satisfactory. It's early days and a low-grade fever might be expected. But we will run some more tests to exclude an infection.' He gently touched the man's shoulder. 'Do you mind if I examine your abdomen?'

Signore Degano nodded, and the nurse pulled the privacy curtains around the bed.

Marco peeled back the sheet. Elena's assessment of the long vertical laparotomy wound was accurate. There didn't appear to be any superficial infection. When he gently palpated the rest of the abdomen, he found it largely soft, suggesting any leakage of enzymes from the pancreas was minimal and localised.

'Well done, Signore,' he said, pulling the sheet back into place. 'I came to see you last night after the surgery but you were asleep, and I wanted to let you rest.'

The patient nodded again and croaked out a hoarse thank you.

'As I explained to your wife last night,' Marco continued, 'the surgery went well. Extremely well, in fact, although it took a little longer than I had expected. The tumour appeared to be confined to the head of the pancreas, as indicated by your scans. But we need to wait for the pathology report for definite results of spread and tumour grade. Your job is to rest but also, when you are able, to get out of this bed with the help of the physiotherapist. Maybe the day after tomorrow we will have you drinking some water and if all goes well we can remove the nasogastric tube and the drip.'

Degano nodded once more and Marco continued. 'Dr Mancini is going to take some blood tests from you now. I will be back to see you later today.'

With one final look at Elena, who was once more smiling fondly at the patient, Marco left her to run the tests. Momentarily free to once more postulate his absurd need for the last thing he wanted—a wife—tingles of excitement and satisfaction flooded his system. What better way to keep romantic feelings out of a relationship than with active dislike and existing distrust? What better way to protect himself from once more choosing the wrong woman than to embrace the risk and marry the one woman who would want nothing to do with him, nothing from him, apart from the only thing he could give her—a business deal? Congratulating himself on his flash of genius, he headed for his outpatient clinic, a renewed spring in his step as the details of his plan fell perfectly into place.

After a day spent in the outpatients pre-op clinic seeing both Dr Caruso's and Dr Brienza's patients, Elena received a summons to Marco's office. At his door, she ran a hand over her hair, tucking a stray lock that had escaped from her ponytail behind her ear as her stomach twisted with trepidation. If he was going to fire her, she wanted to appear calm and collected.

She knocked, going over her outburst the night before. It had been unprofessional. But she'd never met a man who pushed her buttons as effectively as Marco Caruso.

His deep voice invited her to enter and Elena pushed open the door.

'You wanted to see me, Dr Caruso?' Resisting

the urge to glance around his spacious and inviting office, to drool over the stunning views of the island, the sea and the mainland beyond, she held his stare. She had bigger concerns than the impressive beauty of Capri.

'Close the door, please, Dr Mancini.' He stood and when Elena turned after obeying his command, he offered her a seat.

Expecting a delayed reprimand for last night's outburst or, worse, a brutal termination speech, Elena sat, her expression defiant, her back straight and her hands clasped together in her lap.

'How is Signore Degano this evening?' he asked, catching her off-guard. He paced over to the window rather than re-taking his seat behind the desk. He'd removed his suit jacket, his white shirt caressing his muscular arms and broad shoulders.

She shuddered at her body's traitorous reaction and looked away. She had been single since her split from Rocco. The humiliation and damage to her trust… Maybe this inconvenient attraction to the most unsuitable man on earth was the price she had to pay for ignoring her personal life.

'His condition is unchanged,' she said. 'His observations are stable and blood tests as good as can be expected. He's mildly dehydrated so I have instructed the nursing staff to increase his intravenous fluids.'

'Good. Good.' He slid his hands into his trouser pockets and glanced out of the window as if studying his enviable view. In profile, pensive and enigmatic, he seemed more aloof and unreachable than ever. Not that Elena was interested in any kind of connection, even if Marco Caruso was capable of it, which she very much doubted.

She was a loyal daughter, and she did not like this man.

Elena waited, snatching her gaze away from his sexily toned backside.

'Following our…conversation last night—' he began and Elena held her breath, her pulse throbbing, expecting the next words out of his mouth to be *I have formally complained to Personnel about your rudeness and unprofessional behaviour* '—I have a proposition for you,' he finished, turning to face her once more so she flushed from the intensity of his dark stare and the shock of his words.

'Okay…' Elena frowned, her pulse surging. But she was unable to read a single thing from his blank expression.

'We have, I think, successfully proved that there is a certain lack of trust between us and our families.' He spoke without displaying a single emotion, not even the anger he'd momentarily shown the night before when she'd pointed out that the Mancinis had come off worst after the scandal. 'But I have no desire to play the blame game, nor do I think the hospital the correct arena for such pointless recriminations.'

Elena swallowed and waited, hating that so far,

he made perfectly good points. But for her fatigued and momentary slip last night when she'd raised the subject of the hospice both families co-owned, she too had no desire to rake over their fathers' unfortunate past friendship. It was bad enough that she had to see Marco Caruso every day, knowing how his father had betrayed hers, their partnership and their friendship.

'We must temporarily,' he continued, 'work together while you are a locum here, and as you have probably now had a chance to confirm, there is plenty of work to be done at SMC.'

Elena nodded half-heartedly. Not because he was wrong about the workload. But around this man, suspicious seemed to be her default. And he'd yet to state his proposition. 'I agree,' she said. 'But if you do not plan to fire me for my rude outburst last night, what is it that you do want, Dr Caruso?' There was a certain freedom in knowing where she stood with this man. His opinion of her was clearly so low, the only way was up.

'My grandfather Caruso recently passed,' he said in the same carefully controlled voice he used with his patients.

'I'm sorry for your loss,' she automatically replied, to which he waved a hand dismissively.

He stepped closer, his gaze unwavering. 'I am set to inherit the Caruso estate here on Capri from him.'

'Congratulations,' she said, stopping just shy of rolling her eyes at his good fortune. Unlike the Caruso family, generational wealth was an insulation her father lacked. 'But what does that have to do with me?' Regretting that she'd sat down, thus giving him the advantage of standing over her, Elena shifted in the seat. She was bordering on being impolite again, but this conversation seemed to be veering into personal territory.

'Last night you said the Mancini Foundation wished to own the Dignità Hospice, the one remaining and successful investment our fathers made together, outright.'

Elena huffed. 'Successful for Caruso Enterprises in particular, given that you hold the greater share.'

He raised one shoulder in a casual shrug. 'It's my understanding that my father not only made the greater investment, but also put robust legal protections in place to ensure the hospice stayed in trust, thus protecting it from being sold as part of the ensuing civil settlement brought against Medicina dell'Apparenza.'

Elena reluctantly bit her tongue, unable to argue that between their fathers, Dario Caruso was the better businessman.

'You said our business was surgery and our patients,' she pointed out. 'Why is this, your inheritance, relevant to our work? And why are you raising the topic here at the hospital?'

His brief wince gave her a surge of pleasure. 'Our business *is* our patients,' he said. 'And if I may, I will get to the point. My younger sister now heads

Caruso Enterprises. I spoke with her last night about the sale of the Dignità Hospice. I am willing to gift the Mancini Foundation the Caruso stake, but there's something I want in return. Assuming that you are single.'

Elena was out of her chair in a heartbeat. 'And what is that?' she fired back, her breathing accelerating and her hands curled into fists.

He was attractive. Sexy even, in a powerful and virile way, but there were limits to what she'd do to best this man and his family.

'Calm down,' he said, stepping in her direction.

'Calm down?' She huffed. 'I am not for sale.'

For the first time since she'd met him, a flicker of amusement twitched his lips, taking at least five years off his age. 'It is not what you are imagining.' His voice was infuriatingly serene.

'Then enlighten me,' she snapped, eager to be done with this cryptic conversation, to get away from him and the confusing hold he seemed to have over her physically.

His stare, locked on hers, darkened. A muscle twitched in his jaw as if he might regret the next thing that came from his mouth.

Elena's pulse accelerated in the long pause, her throat drying as she waited.

Then he spoke in that same detached voice she found so…infuriating.

'I want you to marry me.'

CHAPTER FOUR

MARCO WATCHED ELENA'S expression pale as her shock turned to horror, finally settling on amused disbelief, which brought the lovely flush of pink back to her cheeks.

'Are you crazy?' she asked with a snort of laughter. 'Why on earth would I ever do that? We can barely stand to be in the same room as each other.'

Marco stepped closer, fascinated by her hazel eyes which he had come to recognise displayed her every emotion, no matter how she tried to oppose him or conceal her feelings. She had spirit, he would give her that. A trait that would serve her well as a surgeon in the long run.

'You want the hospice,' he said softly, fighting his natural inclination towards compassion for this woman and her family. 'I'm afraid that, like all of my father's investments, the stake in Dignità must stay within the Caruso Enterprises trust and therefore in the Caruso family. If you marry me, you will be a Caruso. Temporarily. And the shares can be transferred to you to do with as you please.'

She frowned, her jaw slack with disbelief.

He went on. 'You will receive the Caruso Enterprises' stake in the hospice as a wedding gift. In return, you agree to stay married to me for a period of six months. After that we will divorce.'

'You're actually serious.' She shook her head, as if astounded by his arrogance, her frown deepening. 'And what do *you* get out of such an outrageous arrangement? One which, by the way, I would never entertain for many reasons.'

Marco shrugged, eager to hide his desperation for her agreement in case she refused out of spite or because of their families' history. 'I must be currently married in order to inherit the Caruso estate. Some historical clause in the will the lawyers assure me there is no way around, unfortunately.'

Her lips curved into a cunning and mocking smile. 'And there is no eager woman waiting in the wings, desperate to be the next Signora Caruso? No one else you can blackmail into being your fake wife?'

'No,' he replied. None that suited him anyway. But her words pricked at that dark undercurrent of guilt he'd struggled with since he'd formed the idea of circumventing the legacy cause. He was desperate, not that he wanted her to know that. 'Believe me, having been married once before, I wish I could avoid such drastic measures.'

But this time he would have everything laid out legally to protect his family's legacy so there could be no repeat of the Bianca situation.

'I bet you do,' she muttered, obviously seeing him and his motivation to avoid another messy emotional divorce clearly. 'But surely there must be someone else you could ask. A lover, girlfriend, someone who might be captivated by your…charms.'

When he only pressed his lips together, she continued. 'We dislike each other. We don't even trust each other. And more to the point—' she stepped closer in challenge '—I too am happily single, thank you very much.'

But something in her eyes, the way they shifted, told him she was considering it, despite her many objections. Maybe she too was desperate to resolve the issues of the past.

'We do not need to trust or like each other for this to be beneficially rewarding,' Marco said reasonably, his respect for her growing. 'In fact, it is better this way. Everything will all be drawn up legally in a pre-nuptial agreement. It will be a marriage in name only.'

'Of course it will,' she muttered.

'Six months will be enough time for probate,' he continued, reluctant to explain his caution, because that would mean admitting the mistake he'd made with his first marriage and how Dario had bailed him out at time when he should have been focused solely on his cancer treatment. 'Then you are free to divorce me. Our families' partnership will be severed completely, something that I'm sure will satisfy everyone and draw a line under the entire sorry association with something, at least, salvaged.'

Her stunning eyes narrowed, and another flicker

of respect for her struck him, pleasure in the knowledge that she also had a fiery side. Generally, she smiled too much. Not with him, of course, but he'd spied her often enough laughing with a patient to put them at ease or with the nurses simply because she seemed to have a natural way of finding common ground with people. Swallowing, he brushed aside that pang of frustration he felt at not being a recipient of her smile.

'Obviously,' he went on, 'it will be a purely practical solution to both our problems. A business deal if you like. Although I will add there are other, minor, stipulations.'

'Such as?' she asked, placing her hands on her hips, a move that pulled her blouse tight across her breasts.

The woman was utterly fearless.

'We must attempt to give the appearance that we are madly in love.' Marco discreetly swallowed, keeping his gaze away from her astounding body. 'There will be a quick private wedding ceremony and you must move into the Caruso estate, at least while you are on Capri.'

'Live together?' she asked with another incredulous snort.

'Of course.' He shrugged. 'If we are married, it would look suspicious for you to live anywhere else, at least until you finish your locum position here. But don't worry. The estate has a guest house you can use. You will hardly see me, which will, no doubt, be attractive given our inability to occupy the same room.'

'How convenient,' she quipped, glancing down at the floor. 'Anything else I should know before I consider your startlingly romantic proposal?' Her stare met his once more and he faltered at the hint of vulnerability lurking in the depths of her hazel eyes.

Recalling her age—twenty-eight—he winced guiltily. What woman in her twenties would celebrate such a cold and calculating proposal? He could only hope that her dislike for him, for his family, and her desire to reclaim the one investment their fathers had made together was enough to overcome her other reservations.

'Yes,' he said, ignoring the way the evening sun streaming through the window richened the colour of her glossy dark hair. 'It is best if we keep this arrangement to ourselves. If word gets out that we are married, we risk press speculation and renewed reporting on the Medicina dell'Apparenza scandal, something we would both be keen to avoid, I assume.'

'You assume correctly. Although I personally have nothing to hide and stand by my father and his past decisions, he is not a well man. If I did this, married you, I could never tell him, nor would you want your name publicly associated with a Mancini, I'm sure.' Her smile was taunting.

Marco inclined his head, wondering what illness had befallen Gio Mancini. But he needed to say everything he wanted to say, before he became side-tracked. 'I will, of course, need to confide in my sister Gin as Chief Executive of Caruso Enterprises. She will handle the handover of Dignità shares. But I assure you she is professional and discreet. And if you agree, you will also need to confide in your brother, Dino, of course.'

Her eyes shifted with doubt. She was obviously eager for *no one* to know of any potential connection between them and he understood why. He too would swear Gin to secrecy. He would not want to cause his mother any more pain and she would not understand that this relationship would have nothing to do with feelings.

'But understand this,' he pressed on. 'The Dignità Hospice will be the sum total of any property settlement upon our divorce. The Caruso estate has been in my family for centuries. My immediate family, my mother and sister, each live there for part of the year in separate residencies. You must sign the prenuptial agreement denouncing any future claim to property upon our divorce.'

'Did you whisper such sweet nothings to your first wife?' she said with a smirk. 'No wonder there is no queue of women lining up to be temporarily Signora Caruso.'

'My ex is the reason that this part of our arrangement is non-negotiable,' Marco said, amused by her backbone. 'And it goes without saying, but I will say it anyway: there is no place in this marriage for feelings of any kind.'

He'd learned the hard way how quickly love could sour, how fickle people's motivations. Bianca had once celebrated being part of his family, only to try and tear it down the moment she chose to walk away from their marriage, which sadly happened to coincide with the most unimaginably painful time for them all.

She huffed. 'It's not like there's any chance of that from my perspective. Not with *you*.'

Marco concealed another smile of respect. 'Good. And lastly—'

'Of course there is more,' she interrupted with a snort.

'There is to be no further mention of our personal lives, both past and present, at work. For the duration of your locum position at SMC, and while we are within these walls, we will remain polite and professional and focused on patient care at all times.'

'I am always polite and professional, at least I was until I met you.' Fire flared in her irises as she fisted her hands on her curvaceous hips. 'It's not me proposing a fake marriage to a junior colleague in the workplace.' Her lips pursed as if she was barely holding back from saying more.

'You are correct,' Marco said with a wince, admiring her ability to stay vaguely respectful, especially when she made a very valid point. 'I am aware that I am older than you. That as a consultant I am also partly responsible for your surgical supervision along with Dr Brienza.' A rumble of unease at his duplicity tensed his muscles. But the end would justify the means for them both. For their families, too. 'This will be the last time we ever discuss something non-work-related here,' he promised.

After staring for what felt like a long time, she raised her chin and rolled back her shoulders. 'In that case, I'll think about your comprehensive proposition. Goodnight, Dr Caruso.'

She turned away from him and some panicked impulse saw him reaching for her arm. 'Wait.'

She paused, glancing down to where his fingers encircled her upper arm, just below the short sleeve of her blouse. Marco released her, brushing aside the unwanted impression of soft and warm silky skin, of the intoxicating hint of some feminine perfume she wore, of the soft gasp she'd uttered the moment they'd touched.

'Don't think for too long,' he warned, his chest tight from the power she held over him in that moment. The power to veto his plan and some unanticipated hold over him physically. He hadn't expected an attraction to his fake wife-to-be. But it was nothing he couldn't handle. After all, he rarely abandoned his goals and the stakes—protecting his family's legacy and honouring his father—had never been more pressing. He would simply stay away from her as much as was humanly possible.

'This is a time-sensitive offer,' he continued, an inexplicable tightness in his throat. 'Can I suggest you take the weekend and accept or decline by Monday morning?'

'Very well.' She looked up at him, her frown back.

Something close to doubt pulsed through him, gone in a heartbeat. Maybe she thought him cold and calculating, and maybe she was right. But having been unable to help his father in life, he would honour him in death. He would finish the Caruso Cancer Centre. He'd promised.

Marco stepped back, out of the intimacy of her personal space, and plucked a business card from his desk, handing it over. 'So you can contact me in private with your decision.'

She glanced at the card, which contained his home address and contact info, took one final look at him and left his office without another word.

Marco stared after her for a moment, expecting frustration or even anger that she now held his fate in the palm of her hand. But as he turned back to his desk, resolved to stick to every part of his plan, including ignoring his attraction to Elena Mancini, he realised he wore instead a small impressed smile.

CHAPTER FIVE

AFTER A SLEEPLESS night where she'd replayed that shocking conversation over and over again in her mind, Elena emerged from the shower on Saturday morning resolved. Following her initial shock at his proposal yesterday, the longer Marco had talked, the more sense this deal had made. In accepting it, she had nothing beyond her dignity to lose and everything to gain. A resolution to the unfortunate connection with the Caruso family. The acquisition of the Dignità Hospice for the Mancini Foundation, the not-for-profit organisation her older brother, Dino, had founded after leaving university. Peace of mind for her dear dying Papà, who would end his days knowing that one of his investments had weathered the bankruptcy storm and would make a difference. Knowing that he'd made mistakes in the past, but could leave behind something positive for the future.

Packing an overnight bag, Elena left her rented apartment near SMC and took a taxi to the address on the card that Marco had handed her, her stomach tight and palms clammy. She didn't want her decision playing on her mind all weekend. She was leaving for Naples on the afternoon ferry. It was Gio

Mancini's birthday and the entire family would be visiting him at the hospice. Her mother had even made a birthday cake.

Besides, she and Marco had already agreed to keep their personal conversations away from the hospital.

At the Caruso estate, which was perched high on the hillside overlooking Capri town, she located the intercom beside an ornate set of iron gates and buzzed.

'*Sì*,' a voice said, dragging Elena's gaze from the glimpses of the estate visible through the bars of the gate.

'I'm here to see Dr Caruso. I'm a colleague of his from the hospital.' Of course Marco lived here, his *home* one of many secluded, affluent hideaways dotted across the hillsides of Capri, many of which were owned by wealthy celebrities and successful entrepreneurs.

'Please wait inside the gates,' the female voice instructed.

The automatic lock disarmed and Elena ducked inside the stunning walled estate, lush with mature gardens and abundant birdsong, regarding it bitterly. She tried her best to be unimpressed, but couldn't help but take it all in like a child with their nose pressed to the window of a toyshop. To her left was a pretty cottage, a larger, grander bougainvillea-draped villa some distance away beyond the stone pine trees which provided cool puddles of shade against the morning sun. The warm air was scented with lemon blossom and lavender and sweet mimosa.

But she didn't have long to wait and seethe over their differing fortunes. A man on a golf-style buggy appeared from behind the cottage and pulled up beside her.

'Welcome to the Caruso estate,' the man said. 'My name is Enzo. I am the estate guardian. I will take you to Dr Caruso.'

Elena climbed aboard the buggy, her insides trembling with nerves. Last night, with his outrageous proposal hers to accept or decline, Elena had felt some small restoration of the power imbalance between them. But now, here at his breathtaking home on one of the most beautiful and exclusive islands in the world, she suddenly felt her confidence waver. After a short and winding drive they came to a halt in a cobbled courtyard. The awe-inspiring sight of the azure sea that came into view stole her breath and further rattled her resolve to meet Marco Caruso on her terms. To take what she wanted from this deal, their marriage, and then walk away. Could she pull this off? Focus on the goal while living there and fighting the feeling that she was betraying her family?

'He's in the gym,' Enzo said, indicating a narrow flight of stone steps in the corner of the courtyard. 'It's on the terrace below. You can leave your bag in the buggy if you prefer. It will be quite safe.'

Elena nodded and strode towards the steps, ignoring the astounding vistas in every direction as her determination grew. As her ballet flats clipped on each step her annoyance and bitterness built. While the Mancinis had lost almost everything—their reputation, their family home, her father's health—the Caruso family had all of this and more. At the bottom of the steps she turned away from the view and came to an abrupt halt. Sucked in a gasp. Her pulse flying.

Across another small patio stood a single-storey stone building that appeared carved into the limestone cliff. The sliding doors were open, gauzy curtains billowing in the breeze. The interior boasted a fully equipped gym where Marco worked out. Shirtless, his back to her as he used a lat pulldown weights machine, his near naked body was the epitome of virile male beauty.

Frozen by the sight of his sweat-covered bronzed skin and the well-defined slabs of his deltoids, trapezius and latissimus dorsi muscles, Elena watched with her mouth hanging open, her blood on fire. Every physical aspect of the hateful man was magnificent from his dark, often unruly, hair to his imposing height and manly build. Even his taut muscular backside in workout shorts was…delicious.

Her attraction was utterly irrelevant, to both their deal and because Rocco's betrayal had seriously damaged her ability to trust men. But her body, starved of affection and sex for the past two years, reacted violently to the sight of his near nakedness. Her legs weakened, her temperature increased and she struggled to suck in air without panting as if on heat.

She hesitated, reconsidering her decision to accept Marco's dangerous proposal. He was the enemy and agreeing would make her his wife. She could strive to keep her attraction to him at bay, steer clear of him unless absolutely necessary, but that meant constantly keeping her guard up. The only saving grace was that she need only live there for the duration of her locum position. In a few weeks she could escape back to Naples and live out the rest of their *marriage* away from Marco, his raw sex appeal and the reminders of betrayal simply looking at him roused. The idea that Dino's foundation might be gifted the hospice was so tantalising. The one thing that might be salvaged from her father's entire sorry association with Dario Caruso.

Decided anew, she clipped her way rapidly across the patio before she lost her nerve again. She entered the air-conditioned shade of the gym, loudly clearing her throat to announce her presence. The sooner she told him her decision, the sooner she could get away from him and rediscover her perspective.

'Dr Caruso,' she called. Her voice broke slightly on his name, a misstep that felt like another betrayal to her family so her cheeks stung with shame.

He released the bar of the weight's machine and

turned to face her, reaching for a towel to wipe the sweat from his face.

'Dr Mancini,' he said, tugging the earbuds from his ears. 'To what do I owe this visit?'

He made no attempt to cover his body and Elena locked her stare to his, forbidding it to drop any lower. She stood tall, fighting the urge to fidget as he stared back. His cool gaze swept the length of her body, which was clad in skinny jeans and a simple summer top, making her overheat.

'I have considered your proposal,' she began, pleased with the clarity of her voice this time, 'and wanted to let you know that I accept. I didn't want to wait until Monday and thought this conversation was better carried out away from the hospital.'

'I agree, but you could have just called. I gave you my personal number.'

Elena flushed, raising her chin. 'I think face to face is better, given I have a condition of my own to add to the negotiation.'

'Which is?' he asked, his stare narrowing slightly as he tossed the towel aside and stepped closer, his arms crossed over that broad, sweat-glistened chest as if squaring up for battle.

Was that an amused twitch of his lips?

Elena took a deep breath, ignoring the way his sexy body filled her vision. The man also ground her gears. 'You rein in the animosity at work. Allow me to do my job without your unfounded suspicions,' she said, her pulse buzzing at her own audacity in addressing a senior colleague this way.

She shuddered at the return of power she held in that moment. He was older than her, a senior colleague and her boss. He lived at this enviable estate thanks to his family's success. Whereas she still hesitated to tell new people her name in case they recalled the scandal and judged both her father and her. Marco normally held all the power in their dynamic so she would enjoy every second of negotiating for what she wanted.

'I understand why you may not like me or trust me personally because I'm a Mancini, but I take my work very seriously,' she continued when he only narrowed his eyes and stared as if fascinated. 'I have always wanted to be a surgeon, like my father. I won't have this…arrangement interfering with my career in any way. As for the rest of this—' she waved her arm to indicate the lavish estate '—with the exception of the Dignità Hospice, I want absolutely nothing else from you.'

'That's what my ex-wife said,' he muttered darkly.

Curiosity piqued at this personal crumb of information, Elena ignored his cynical comment and continued, 'What I do want, however, is to feel that my locum job is secure for its duration.'

'I'm not going to fire my own wife, Elena,' he said, a definite smile on his lips as he regarded her so intently *she* felt naked.

Rather than inflame her further as she might have

guessed, the gesture and the way he said her name only added to his outrageous attractiveness. Away from the hospital, he seemed different. Still ruthless and demanding but also something more. Or maybe it was simply the lack of clothing frying her brain's synapses.

'I'm only here for a matter of weeks, but I want it to be a valuable experience, to learn from your and Dr Brienza's surgical expertise,' she went on, 'to do my job unhindered by prejudice. I want you to treat me like any other locum registrar. If it helps, just pretend I am someone else and not a Mancini.'

'Very well,' he said, his brooding stare so curiously watchful she wished she knew what he was thinking. 'Any other requests?'

'No,' she said, sagging with relief. *Other than put a shirt on, perhaps...*

In spite of herself, her gaze fell again to his chest and then drifted lower. To the dark strip of hair that bisected his ridged abdomen and disappeared into the waistband of his low-slung workout shorts. They were loose and concealed a tantalising bulge, his strong muscular thighs as tanned and toned as the rest of him.

Aware she was staring, she flushed and looked up.

'Enjoying the view?' His dark eyes glittered with what appeared to be amusement and triumph and, as if emerging from behind the shadow of cloud into bright sunlight, a broad smile tugged at his decadent lips.

'No,' she lied, flushing harder.

His sensual mouth twisted with a knowing smile. 'In that case, I agree to your stipulation.'

'Good,' she croaked, wishing she'd never set foot inside his beautiful estate. She turned for the door, desperate to leave before he saw how badly she fancied him.

'Shall we shake on it?' he called after her, causing her to spin around. Another flicker of amusement danced on his lips.

Elena stared at the hand he held out as if it were a tarantula. She didn't want to touch him. Not when he was practically naked. When he'd noticed her admiring his body. When he wore that look of intrigued amusement as if he knew exactly how their chemistry affected her. But nor would she have him believe she was afraid. She took his hand, her pulse flying, shook firmly once.

She made it to the door this time before he spoke again and she halted for a second time.

'Tell me,' he drawled, 'if surgery has always been your dream, why did you take a break from your specialist registrar training? I've read your CV. Why are you currently doing locum work when you should be on a surgical training scheme, earning your stripes and sitting your professional exams?'

Elena hesitated, reluctant to tell him anything more than he needed to know. Not that she had anything to hide. And his observation and the hidden implication that her actions belied her dedication to her career crushed any residual physical attraction she felt for him like a rose petal underfoot.

'Because I love my family,' she said, not bothering to hide the emotion from her voice or the challenging tilt of her chin. 'After the closure of Medicina dell'Apparenza, my father was diagnosed with Parkinson's disease. I decided to take a temporary break from my training to help out as much as I could with his care. I am a good daughter and love my papà dearly, so the sacrifice was an easy one to make.'

'I see.' He frowned, any trace of humour gone. 'My condolences for your father's ill health.'

'Please,' she scoffed. 'You are a Caruso. Your father's son. You don't care one jot for my father.'

His stare hardened and he took another step closer, his intense eyes pinning her in place. 'You think you know me, but you do not.'

He was too close. Too manly. Too dangerous. Standing in the doorway, in the glare of the sun, she broke out in a sweat.

But she dug in her heels. 'I know you are arrogant and ruthless and cold,' she said, the frustration she'd battled since coming to work for him once more spilling free, maybe because she really wanted to flee. 'Even with your patients.'

Marco's dark eyes glittered darkly as if he saw through her. 'I focus on outcomes not flattery.' He stepped closer still so she had to raise her chin to maintain eye-contact. 'All my patients want from me,' he continued, 'is more years with their loved ones. That is all that matters. That is exactly what I try to give them, exactly where I concentrate my efforts.'

A flood of shame washed over her, raising fresh heat to her cheeks. 'You can still do your job and be approachable. You don't have to be so…robotic.' Aware she'd lost her temper, she pressed her lips together. He could still fire her even if they *were* married, although now that she'd negotiated her term that would negate their agreement.

His eyes narrowed and her breathing sped up. This close, she was bathed in the heat and masculine scent of his semi-naked body.

'I prefer results,' he said, his stare dipping to her mouth as if she might interrupt. 'Patient survival outcomes. Otherwise, how else could I face relatives like you? The ones who know the pain of watching a loved one deteriorate before their very eyes?'

Elena stayed silent, hating that he made a good point. Hating that her body reacted to his closeness, heat sliding through her like honey.

'The only thing worse than delivering the news that a disease is terminal,' he said in his doctor's voice, 'is being the recipient of that news about someone you love. Wouldn't you agree?'

Elena swallowed past her hot achy throat. He was right about what patients and relatives facing a life-limiting diagnosis wanted. Every day was precious when every visit might be the last. That was why she went to Naples whenever she could.

'I have to go,' she said, stepping back so she could breathe. 'I will see you on Monday morning at the hospital. I trust you will put things in place for our… wedding. Just let me know when and where.'

After all, it wasn't a real wedding and Marco had everything already figured out anyway. A watertight pre-nup. A six-month convenient marriage. No feelings and a quickie divorce. Such a cold, emotionless union to a stranger wasn't how she'd envisioned her wedding day would be back when she'd thought she would marry Rocco. But that hadn't eventuated. He'd let her down. Betrayed her when she'd needed him most. Now she simply wanted to get her fake nuptials to this man over and done with.

'I will.' The look he gave her was once more expressionless.

She nodded and at last walked away. After all, there was nothing more to say. They had made their deal, for better or for worse.

The next day, when his phone rang after eight p.m. on Sunday evening, Marco was surprised to see the call was from Elena. He'd spent the entire weekend thinking about her after her visit and acceptance of his proposal. The way she'd looked at him with both hunger and distaste. The names she'd called him and her confusion when he'd defended himself. She obviously did not know that his father had passed, and he had no current desire to enlighten her. She thought she was the only one grieving. That her family was the only one to suffer. Let her bask in that ignorance and self-righteousness. As long as she stuck to their agreement.

'Dr Mancini,' he said, his memory of her from the day before fresh in his mind.

She'd looked younger in her casual clothes. Her beauty more obvious with her long rich brown hair down around her shoulders and her sexy body outlined by casually feminine clothing. Despite all the distrust and animosity swirling, it had taken every scrap of his willpower not to stare at her curves and the freckles dotting her chest.

'Dr Caruso. Sorry to call you at home,' she said, her voice tinged with urgency, 'but I thought you'd want to know. It's Signore Degano. His condition is deteriorating.'

'I'll be there in five minutes,' Marco said and ended the call, hurrying outside to his car parked on the drive. Within seven minutes he was striding onto the high dependency ward towards Degano's bed.

Elena was at the bedside when he arrived, dressed in a similar way as she'd been yesterday as if she'd unofficially popped in to see the patient on her day off.

'Signore Degano,' he said, reaching for the man's

pulse as he glanced at the monitor recording his blood pressure and oxygen saturation.

His pulse was rapid but regular and his blood pressure low. Someone, probably Elena, had inserted a second intravenous cannula and a saline infusion.

'The abdomen is tender,' Elena said, drawing back the covers to expose the patient's wound. 'And there's blood in three of the drains. I've ordered an urgent CT angiogram.'

Marco nodded and gently examined Degano's abdomen. 'I don't think there's time to wait for a scan,' he said, one eye on the low blood pressure reading. 'Have you done the blood work? Ordered a cross match for a transfusion if required?'

'Yes.' She nodded, her teeth nibbling at her bottom lip with concern.

'Fredo,' he addressed the patient, 'we think you might be bleeding internally. Sometimes a ligation on a blood vessel can work free. We need to take you back to Theatre, I'm afraid, and have a look, if you consent.'

The man nodded and, without waiting, Marco and Elena pushed his bed from the ward towards the lifts down to Theatre.

Two hours later, after locating the source of the bleeding—the ligated gastro-duodenal artery—Marco and Elena de-gowned, tiredly tossing their surgical robes into the laundry bin and their hats, masks and gloves into the trash.

They washed up at the sinks outside the operating room, each of them quiet now that the adrenaline of the emergency surgery had faded. Marco noticed the late hour and winced, glancing sideways to see that Elena looked tired. 'You should get home. I'll check on him before I do the same.'

She nodded, glancing his way, her eyes dull and guilty. 'I'm sorry,' she said, her voice flat with fatigue. 'For what I said yesterday in your gym.' She faced him, her chin up as she met his stare. 'You are a good surgeon, and of course you care about your patients.'

Marco pulled some paper towels from the dispenser and dried his hands. Her accusations had stung at the time of course. Not because he gave less than a hundred and ten percent to his work. But because the one time he hadn't been in control, hadn't been able to hold the scalpel himself, the outcome had taken his father from him.

'Why were you even here tonight?' he asked, frustrated that he cared about her obvious fatigue and the way she was looking at him as if she was re-evaluating what she knew. 'You are not on call.'

She looked down, shaking the water from her hands. 'I popped into the hospital on my way home from the ferry. I wanted to check on Signore Degano. I arrived on the ward just as things began to deteriorate.'

Marco frowned, surprised anew by her dedication. 'You were on the mainland this weekend?' he asked, some irritation at the back of his neck raising the fine hairs there.

'Yes,' she said. 'I took a ferry back from Naples this evening.'

Images of her from the day before and from earlier when he'd first walked onto the ward this evening flashed in his mind. Fresh, lovely, a beautiful woman in her late twenties. Heat flooded his veins, attraction and a pointless slug of possessiveness. She'd claimed to be single when he'd first mentioned his marriage plan, but of course there must be a man in her life. She was a stunning, sexy woman. Intelligent and engaging, with a smile that could break the most jaded of spirits.

It was none of his business what she did in her time off, but for this fake marriage to work, there could be no…distractions. For either of them.

Tossing the paper towels into the bin, Marco crossed his arms over his chest, refusing to analyse the burn behind his sternum. 'It is nothing to do with me currently, but if you have a lover in Naples, you might consider temporarily giving him up for appearances' sake. After next week, after we are married, we cannot do anything that might interfere with the perception that we are a couple in love.'

Elena dropped her towels into the bin after his and turned to face him with her hands on her hips, her fatigued stare resolute and challenging. 'Does that work for both of us? Six months is a long time. I cannot be expected to abstain if my so-called husband is free to do as he pleases. No one who knows me would believe I would tolerate such an unequal marriage.'

Marco kept his voice steady and controlled, even when he wanted to smile that she continued to put him in his place. 'We agreed to keep our marriage to ourselves, with the exception of the lawyers of course and Gin and Dino. But yes, the abstinence applies to us both.'

'Good,' she said, staring back with challenge.

'Will it be a problem for you?' he asked, telling himself his interest was purely practical. For their ruse to work, it had to appear convincing. But why was she single? Were the rest of the Italian population of men stupid and blind?

'No problem,' she replied vaguely. 'I have been single for a while, and outside of my arrangement with you have no desire to change that status. Relationships require loyalty and take trust. I, like my father, have learned the hard way that you freely dispense that at your peril.'

'Someone hurt you?' he asked, ignoring the jibe about Dario betraying Gio, although it was more of a statement. He could read those dark eyes of hers as easily as he read human anatomy. She was young. Beautiful. Smart. What else but a broken heart would make her choose the single life? But why did he care?

'Why would I tell you that?' she asked, adding when he stayed silent, 'Let's just say that bankruptcy and public scandal are a good test of people's loyalty. Words are just words. It is actions that speak the truth.'

Marco kept his expression impassive, even as internally he winced. So the Caruso-Mancini estrangement had cost Elena something personal too. Her family's financial decline, her father's diagnosis and maybe a lost love. Some spineless man who had perhaps valued the unfounded opinions of strangers over the relationship.

Realising that he'd led them into personal territory with his jealous imaginings, Marco looked down and muttered, 'Sometimes even actions are not enough. Sometimes they are taken out of your control.' He was a surgical oncologist. He treated people for cancer every day. And yet he hadn't been able to treat or save his own father.

He swallowed, appalled that he'd forgotten himself. When he looked back, she continued to frown as if waiting for him to elaborate. But they were not friends. They needn't like each other or even trust each other for their plan to work. He was her boss and she'd made it clear what she thought of him since the day they'd met.

'Get some sleep, Dr Mancini,' he said, hardening his heart to the flicker of vulnerability he saw in her eyes. It had been there yesterday, too, when she'd talked about her father's diagnosis and was there again when she'd mentioned her trust issues.

But just like this unrelenting buzz of attraction,

her personal life was not his concern. He needed to stay focused on his own goals: the inheritance and cancer centre.

'Goodnight,' he called and headed for the changing rooms, his eye firmly on the prize—a new hospital in honour of his father—and not his beautiful and disarming soon-to-be wife.

CHAPTER SIX

In keeping with the plausibility of their fake wedding, Elena chose to wear white for the simple civil marriage ceremony the following weekend. She'd paired the white sundress with her favourite nude ballet flats so when she faced Marco before the registrar in the Capri Town Hall he seemed to dwarf her, both physically and with his calm confident presence and unwavering stare.

Elena robotically recited her vows in a similar clear and unemotional voice to Marco. The hollow place in the centre of her chest grieved for her younger self. For the Elena who, by loving Rocco, had made a mistake and fallen for the wrong man. She'd believed he'd loved her back, that she might marry him one day, dreamed of a romance-filled day with their friends and family, and had been devastated and betrayed when, as a journalist, he'd chosen his career over their relationship and loyalty to her and her family.

But *this* was not a real marriage. This was a cold, calculated deal with a man she neither knew or particularly liked.

'These rings are a symbol of the statements you

have made to one another,' the registrar said, handing them over.

Marco slid the gold band first around Elena's finger and she did the same with the second ring, fighting to ignore how handsome he looked in his midnight-blue suit and linen shirt casually open at the neck to reveal a tantalising glimpse of that manly bronzed chest she'd seen in the gym. Seen, drooled over, denied.

'Elena and Marco,' the registrar continued with a smile, 'I now pronounce you are lawfully joined in matrimony. Congratulations.'

Elena smiled her thanks at the registrar and raised her eyes to Marco, expecting to see the same pragmatic and dispassionate expression he'd worn throughout the ceremony. But something else glimmered in his stare, something that made her suck in a barely audible breath as he stepped close and lowered his head, capturing her lips in a decisive but soft kiss.

Elena's pulse leapt, her insides trembling as she battled the shock and thrilling feel of his lips against hers. Soft but commanding. Making her adrenaline spike. Giving her pause, so for a second she kissed him back rather than pull away.

He released her just as quickly, his head lowered to whisper, 'For appearances' sake.'

A cold shower of humiliation drained through her, dousing the languid heat and ignited sparks from his kiss. She stepped back and ducked her head so he wouldn't see her embarrassment. Of course controlled, unemotional Marco was only thinking of putting on a good show. Whereas for a second, because despite it all she was deeply attracted to him, Elena hadn't been able to stop her body's excited response. Their chemistry had for her been a white-hot spark with all the potential to set alight a blaze, if ever she was stupid enough to fan it into a flame.

But she wasn't stupid, and chemistry could be ignored, especially when it was one-sided.

She looked up and unflinchingly met his stare.

He frowned, his eyes darting between hers as if her reaction to the kiss had confused him. As if he was about to apologise. But that would give away the ruse.

Elena glanced at the celebrant, who after a second's bewildered hesitation, maybe from the newlyweds' rather tame kiss and lack of joy, began to clap, joined by their witnesses.

Elena thanked the celebrant and headed for the door. Marco, right behind her, placed his hand in the small of her back and guided her from the room where she'd sealed her fate.

Married, when she'd vowed after Rocco's betrayal that she would not be hurt again. Married to man she didn't like. Married into a family that had contributed to the shame and ruin of her own.

Resolved, despite what Marco suggested, that she would keep this decision from everyone she knew, including her brother, Elena held her head high as she crossed the expansive marble foyer of the Town Hall, which was occupied by excited couples waiting their turn to be married. Elena ignored their happiness and followed Marco outside, where a car waited to drive them to the Caruso estate.

In the back of the car, Elena sat silently beside Marco, her thoughts tripping over themselves. She had often imagined her wedding to a man she loved, a man who couldn't live without her. That depressing twenty-minute ceremony with two strangers as their witnesses and this man at her side was most certainly not part of her ultimate fantasy.

Holding in a sigh, she visualised the benefits of the choice she had made today. The Dignità Hospice would become a part of the Mancini Foundation. Her father could live out the rest of his days at that very hospice, secure in the knowledge that at least one thing had been salvaged from his dealings with Dario Caruso. And when this was over, when she was free to walk away from her fake husband, the Mancini family would finally be free of the ill-fated association.

'You are already having second thoughts,' Marco said beside her, his calm voice free of judgement, which only grated against her eardrums. 'I think they heard that sigh in Rome.'

Elena looked up, startled that her husband possessed both the emotional intelligence to notice her quiet contemplation and the humanity to care that she might, for a second, mourn her practical, unromantic decision.

'No,' she said on another sigh she couldn't bother to hide. 'Just imagining my next wedding, my next groom. Looking forward to how different it will be. Most definitely *not* for appearances' sake.'

As if of its own accord, Elena's stare dipped to his sexy mouth, waiting for him to voice another quip with which she could find fault. But that only reminded her of the kiss and how it had, for a second, stolen her breath.

'You objected to my kiss,' he stated matter-of-factly, nothing in his expression hinting at his feelings.

'Yes, I did,' she lied, because she hadn't objected until he'd whispered his humiliating justification. She'd been too stunned and then aroused to feel anything but the feel and taste of him and how strongly she had wanted the kiss, at least, to be real where everything else was fake.

'Apologies,' he said tightly, holding her stare. 'Be reassured it was a one-off and won't happen again.'

'Good.' Elena glanced out of the car window, her spirits sinking further despite the stunning summer's day in which Capri sparkled. Suddenly the consequences of her decision, of her actions today, hit full force so she almost gasped. What had she done? No matter how much she'd been hurt in the past, one day she wanted another relationship. A real one. When she was ready to trust again, she wanted a husband and a family. Love, the unshakable kind.

'Why is there no man in your life?' Marco asked quietly, his lips pressed together in a small frown. 'At your age, you should be falling in love, not shackling yourself to a cynical old man in some depressing business deal.'

'Why do you care?' she challenged.

'Was it the man who hurt you?' he asked, completely ignoring her question.

'Maybe I was in love once and realised I'd actually had a lucky escape,' she said, her throat aching at her former blind faith. At how openly she'd given Rocco her entire heart. 'I don't need a man for my happiness. And it will be a long time before I can trust one not to betray and reject me again.' That didn't mean she would always be content with so little.

He frowned. 'But you just said you want to be married again in the future. For real next time.'

'Maybe…' She sighed again. How dare he use her own words against her when she'd intended to use them against him!

'I wish you well with that,' he muttered. He stared for a few beats then waved his hand dismissively. 'But of course, you are young. You have time to find love again, if that is what you want.'

'Isn't that what everyone wants?' Elena watched the bitter curl of his mouth. 'Maybe not *you*,' she added. 'By the time this is over, you will have chalked up two divorces. I take it you're in no hurry to bother risking a third?'

Somehow, talking about the future seemed to minimise what they'd just done. The deception. The joylessness. The danger.

But no matter how pragmatic she was, her stomach churned with doubt. Even sitting in the back of this car with him left her restless and edgy, the memory of that kiss recurring in a loop. She was scared to move in case she strayed too close to him and once more experienced the inescapable heat and fizzle of her physical attraction. How would she deal with living at his home? They would see each other all the time, both in and out of the hospital. There'd be no escape from the way he made her feel… As if she might see more than a handsome, successful, albeit ruthless man if she studied him hard enough. As if she might see his hidden depths. As if it might somehow give the past meaning. Instead, her every interaction with him only left her more confused, as if she could not equate the dedicated and meticulous surgeon with the ruthless son of the man who'd betrayed her father.

'It is not a current priority for me,' he said, glancing out of the window as they climbed the hills above the town. 'I am still smarting from my first divorce.'

'Did she leave you broken-hearted then?' Elena asked, because, like him, she was curious, and now that they'd said *I do*, she had nothing to lose. The game was in play. And by marrying him she'd performed her side of the bargain.

She didn't really know him, couldn't fully trust him, but she trusted him to keep his side of their deal. His stake in this arrangement was perhaps greater than her own. He needed her in order to inherit.

Marco sucked air through his teeth as he stared out at the passing homes on the hill. 'We left each other. That's what you do when something isn't working. You walk away before a bad situation gets any worse.'

'Or you ride the storm together,' she said bitterly in case he was referring to their fathers' medical partnership. 'Communicate. Find common ground, common goals. Work together.'

'My ex-wife and I communicated plenty, I assure you,' Marco said, once more casting an assessing glance her way. 'Like you, she had a fiery side.' His stare dipped to her lips, which were glossed with her favourite lipstick. Maybe he was recalling the accusing words she'd hurled his way that day at his estate. 'But sometimes,' he continued, 'people's motives are not pure. Not what they would have you believe.'

'Very cynically put,' she said, scoffing. Clearly Marco trusted no one. And maybe he had it right.

'You hinted at as much that night we took Signore Degano back to Theatre,' he challenged. 'So you know exactly what I'm talking about.'

'Your ex lied to you?' Elena asked, struggling to believe that she and Marco Caruso had anything in common beyond their work. But it would explain why he was single, why there was no one else he could rope into his charade.

He turned to face her, his stare flinty. 'More that she perhaps lied to herself. She craved the fantasy of marriage to me.' They passed through the electronic gates of the estate and he waved his hand. 'She wanted all of this but eventually tired of being married to a surgeon who worked long, often erratic hours for the good of others. She wanted all of my attention.'

'Did she expect you to give up your career?' she asked, wondering how someone married to Marco could be so blind to his drive and determination.

'Probably. But a surgeon is who I am. You understand that, I'm sure.'

'You don't forgive her for leaving you?' she asked quietly.

They had arrived at the bottom of the long curving drive, the car taking a left and pulling up outside a smaller villa Elena was seeing for the first time.

Marco sat still for a second, then turned to face her. 'I can't forgive her for coming after my family at a time when we were all preoccupied with the court case and the closure of Medicina dell'Apparenza.'

Elena glanced at her lap. 'So we have both made mistakes in the past. Loved the wrong people. People who didn't truly see us. Didn't want who we are.' Having this in common with him gave her no relief. But at least now they understood each other and the motivations that had led them here: married enemies.

'What was your mistake?' he asked when she felt certain the subject was closed.

'I loved someone disloyal,' she said. 'Someone who betrayed me for career advancement rather than stand by me at my lowest point.' Rocco had chosen to report on her father's story, callously choosing his career over their relationship.

'Then you are better off without him.'

'I agree.'

Marco dragged his stare from hers and left the back of the car to open Elena's door. She thanked him and he collected her luggage from the boot. She didn't have much on Capri, but what she'd brought over she'd packed up the night before, leaving her rental empty this morning before the ceremony.

'Welcome to the guest house,' Marco said, leading her in through a side door. 'This has everything you could need,' he added, placing her bags on the tiles in the hallway before crossing the elegant living space towards the open French windows which admitted warm lemon-scented air and the views of another sun-drenched stone terrace and glistening ocean beyond.

'You are, of course, welcome to explore any part of the estate. The pool, the gym, the gardens. Please treat this as your home for the next few weeks while you are working at SMC. The rest of my family are currently in Rome. So it's just the two of us here and the staff.'

Elena nodded, gripping her bare arms although she wasn't cold. But the reality of her situation had fully dawned. She was a prisoner of her own making, her cage gilded, the views breathtaking but also lonely. And nowhere to escape Marco.

'You've…met Enzo, the guardian,' Marco continued, his voice betraying an uncharacteristic hitch of hesitation. 'His wife, Maria, is the housekeeper. Just dial zero from the phone to connect to her for anything you need. She is a typical Italian nonna so will no doubt deliver an endless supply of home-cooked meals. In fact, her pasta dishes are the reason we installed the home gym. If you are able to successfully decline, please let me know how. I haven't been able to achieve that for over forty years.' He shot her an uncertain half-smile.

Elena tried not to imagine the picture he painted. A young Marco running around the estate. What an idyllic and privileged place to grow up.

'Thank you,' she said, suddenly needing her own family's company. Needing people who saw her and understood her and loved her just the way she was.

'Settle in,' he said, casting her a final unreadable glance before leaving the guest house and his new *wife* without a backward glance.

Elena watched him cross the drive and head for another part of the estate, her heart heavy and her emotions scattered. The more she learned about Marco Caruso, the less she understood him. He might be her handsome husband, might spark her desire, physically, but he was also a stranger, a man driven to win at any cost. Just like his father. Since having her heart broken, since being betrayed by the man she'd thought had loved her, she'd struggled to trust any man. But just like she would not need to meet Dario Caruso if he was currently in Rome, she also would not need to trust the man she had married beyond that he would uphold his side of their bargain.

In a few weeks, her locum position would end and she could move back home to Naples. She would never need to see her husband again, not even for the divorce.

CHAPTER SEVEN

On the Monday morning after the wedding, Marco made his way to the pre-op ward, his mood already tense. He hadn't seen Elena since leaving her to settle in at the Caruso estate's guest house on Saturday afternoon. In fact, he'd learned from Enzo that she'd left for the mainland that evening, catching the last ferry to Naples. But just because he'd had the estate to himself didn't mean that his new wife hadn't constantly occupied his thoughts.

He had no right to feel anything about her sneaking away after their wedding. But nor had he been able to stop himself restlessly prowling the property, swimming, visiting the gym, taking lunch and dinner on the terrace, all in the hope of catching a glimpse of her. Even in that she had thwarted him, returning to the estate after dark late last night.

His mind raced—where had she been at the weekend and whom had she been with? Logic told him she was visiting family, but his mind kept returning to other possibilities. That she had a casual lover on the mainland. One who brought out that dazzling smile of hers and soothed her regret over her temporary loveless marriage to him.

Marco walked onto the ward, looked up from

greeting Luisa, the ward receptionist, and spied his wife with Antonio, one of the male nurses. They stood at the bedside of one of Marco's patients, chatting and smiling. He watched, flagellating himself as Elena laughed with both men, who each looked at her entranced as if she were a beautiful and benevolent goddess. And maybe she was. Approachable, professional, largely unjaded by life.

Frustration rumbled inside him. He too felt bewitched by her to some degree. He hadn't planned to kiss her at their wedding ceremony but some strong impulse had overcome him as she'd looked up at him with resignation and a hint of regret over their deception. He'd moved instinctively, drawn to the apparent softness of her full lips. To the well-concealed sparks of fire in her hazel eyes. The moment their lips had touched, desire had roared through him. It was brief, almost dismissively so, but she'd responded, her lips clinging to his as if she'd wanted the kiss to be real. And since that first illicit taste his mind had become consumed by her image, her sweetness, the soft gasp of desire she'd tried to hide.

Holding himself in check now, Marco joined the three of them and the light-hearted conversation immediately ceased. He adjusted his facial expression, smoothing it into something neutral in case he'd actually displayed an accidental frown of disapproval. Was Elena right about him? Was his manner cold and remote? He'd always thought himself merely efficient.

'Signore Nucci.' He shook the patient's hand. 'All ready for your surgery?'

Elena shifted beside him, stepping away to give him space. He caught a waft of that floral perfume she wore and clenched his jaw to ward off the distraction.

'Yes, Dr Caruso.' The older man smiled hesitantly, showing his apprehension.

'Dr Mancini here will be assisting me with your operation today,' Marco told the patient, hoping the news would alleviate some of the patient's nerves.

'Then I am doubly lucky,' Signore Nucci said, glancing between them and smiling at Elena.

'Do you have any questions for me?' Marco asked, quickly checking the man's pulse and glancing at his observations chart, all the while aware of Elena watching the interaction with a small frown.

'No. You have explained everything several times in your clinics,' Nucci replied and Marco nodded.

It was always a balance between giving the patients all the information they needed to make an informed consent without overburdening them with too many technical details of the surgery.

'Good. Then I will see you downstairs.'

With a tilt of his head, Marco motioned for Elena to follow him from the bedside. They had surgical matters to discuss. But also, he hadn't seen her since their wedding. He wanted to ensure she had recovered from the unwanted kiss and her obvious regret. No woman dreamed of such a clinical and loveless wedding, no matter how temporary their marriage might be or how desperate she was to protect herself from future heartbreak.

'Did you have a good weekend?' he surprised himself by asking first, irrationally envious of the plans she'd had no obligation to share with him and feeling guilty that he'd trapped her into a fake marriage, one from which she'd felt compelled to immediately flee.

Her momentary flash of surprise became polite indifference. 'Yes, thank you. You?'

Marco nodded, frustrated by the situation *he* had created. There was obviously little trust between them but, despite her impression of him, he wasn't made of stone. He too had regrets.

'Have you had a chance to review Signore Nucci's case?' he asked. 'His scans and the planned surgery?' He couldn't seem to stop staring at her mouth, recalling the second of soft pressure as she'd kissed him back in front of their celebrant, despite her shock. What had she been thinking in the moment? Did she find him attractive in spite of everything? Was that why she'd kissed him back, or had it simply been a reflex? The way she'd looked at him when he'd pulled back and then quickly dropped her gaze as if embarrassed had shaken his normally rock-solid assurance. But he was eighteen years her senior A workaholic divorcee with grand plans to build his own hospital. Maybe he'd been so caught up in grief for both his father, his grandfather and his dreams for the estate that his awareness of when a woman found him attractive was clouded.

'Yes, I came in early this morning to review all of your patients set for operations today,' she said, her stare filled with curiosity and that mocking flicker of amusement that let him know she would always call him out.

'Good. In that case,' he said, needing to unsettle her as much as she unsettled him, 'maybe it's time to allow you to pick up a scalpel.'

It was his job to supervise and train her, and she'd proved time and time again how dedicated she was to her career, despite the break to help care for her father. Dario Caruso had faded fast after receiving his cancer diagnosis. But had he lingered, Marco too might have made a similar decision to Elena and taken a career break.

Her eyes widened with surprise. 'Okay…'

Frustrated that he was responsible for her hesitation because of his former attitude, he gave her a decisive nod. 'Excellent. I'll see you down there.'

Before he could reveal anything more of his motivations for his sudden change of heart, he left the ward under the weight of his enchanting *wife's* startled stare.

Marco had a full day of surgeries ahead. After Elena had assisted him to perform a straight-forward anterior resection for an adenocarcinoma of the sigmoid colon, they'd taken a quick coffee break and then scrubbed back in. Signore Nucci's operation was next on the list.

Feeling uncertain of Marco's strange mood, Elena fully expected him to rescind his offer that she might operate. After all, their wedding had done nothing to dissipate the wariness and distrust between them. If anything, her moving into the estate had made it worse. She never knew when she might see him and when she was there seemed to look out for him. When they weren't together, he was constantly on her mind. Him and the memory of her reaction to that kiss. Her wild imaginings that if they were ever to kiss for real it would be wild and passionate and lead to more…

That kiss might have been for show, but she could no longer deny that she was deeply attracted to her husband. And if he ever showed any sign of wanting her in return, she might actually be tempted to break their arrangement and sleep with him. A good thing, then, that she was a Mancini and him a Caruso…

Once re-gowned and standing opposite him with the anaesthetised Signore Nucci between them, she almost gaped under her mask when Marco reached for a scalpel and held it out to her, handle first.

'Do you feel confident that you know this case well enough to begin?' he asked, his dark stare unreadable in the gap between his hat and mask.

'Of course.' Elena nodded, quickly recovering and welcoming the chance to operate rather than assist. 'I know your planned surgery is excision of the tumour with as generous a resection margin of normal tissue as possible, given the aim to preserve function of the arm for the patient.'

As she took the proffered scalpel, Marco nodded and clasped his gloved hands before him. 'Then proceed.'

Elena dragged in a deep calming breath. He offered neither an endorsement nor a challenge. But given their former distrust and his warning that she would need to prove herself to him professionally, Elena couldn't help but wonder if the move was an indication of a very small thaw. Or maybe he was simply upholding his side of their bargain to treat her like any other registrar now that they were legally husband and wife.

She felt the weight of the scalpel in her hand. She could do this. Had, in fact, completed this type of operation several times before. Only that had been without perfectionist Marco watching her every move.

Pushing his presence from her mind, Elena leant on her training and with the nod from the anaesthetist that all was ready and with plenty of gauze on hand to clear the field of blood, confidently incised the skin above the tumour, which had been outlined with a marker pen earlier on the ward.

'Good,' Marco said as he watched her progress. 'We know from the scans that the tumour is approximately nine centimetres in diameter at its greatest point. We are expecting it to be close to but not involving the humerus. We know that this tumour is relatively slow growing and from the biopsy reports that it is a well-differentiated liposarcoma.'

Acting in accordance with Marco's preferred surgical approach, Elena carefully dissected a plane between the long and short heads of the biceps brachii muscle in the upper arm. Marco passed her a retractor and as she slipped it into position and opened up the plane between the muscles, the tumour capsule came into view.

'Good,' Marco said. 'You have pretty clear visibility now.'

As Elena slowly dissected the tumour from the surrounding tissues, paying attention to the anatomical landmarks, nerves and blood vessels of the upper arm, Marco held a retractor and watched her closely, offering words of encouragement and the occasional caution.

By the time the cardiac monitor alarm sounded, blaring out a warning, Elena had almost forgotten their former disputes and mistrust even existed, he'd been so supportive.

At the ear-piercing sound, she froze, her gaze flitting first to Marco and then to the anaesthetist.

'It's okay,' Marco told Elena, his hand out as he too looked to the anaesthetist for a clue as to what had transpired.

The anaesthetist made her checks, her stare on the heart's electrical rhythm trace. 'Just a flurry of premature ventricular contractions,' she said. 'But no haemodynamic instability. Blood pressure is stable.'

Marco nodded and glanced back at Elena, whose own heart rate had reacted to the alarm, as was its function. She held his stare, slowly inhaling some deep breaths under her mask, waiting for his instructions.

'It seems to have settled spontaneously,' the anaesthetist said.

'Are you happy for us to proceed?' Marco asked.

'Yes.'

Marco turned to Elena and offered an encouraging nod. 'Carry on.'

Relieved now to have his calm, supportive presence, his years of surgical experience, Elena continued her dissection of the tumour, and the rest of the operation passed without further incident.

It was only later, when she'd ducked away from Theatres to grab some lunch from the cafeteria, that her thoughts returned to her boss—*her husband*—and what his show of faith in her abilities might actually mean. Maybe nothing had changed since they'd become husband and wife. Or maybe, just maybe, it was a small sign of Marco's professional trust in her. It was too much to expect that he could ever trust her outside of work, but the gesture put an extra spring in her step nonetheless.

Progress was progress. As long as she could stop lusting after him…

CHAPTER EIGHT

MARCO OFTEN SWAM in the estate pool in the evenings to clear his head after a long day at work. The repetitive movement of his front crawl, the cool water and the setting sun on his back normally soothed both his body and mind. But tonight, the ritual was unable to stop him thinking of her, his *wife*.

Working with her, having her live on the estate, his thoughts consumed by her lovely smile and sublime body, there was not a moment's escape. He couldn't help but respect her as a doctor. Many registrars would quail under a consultant's blunt instructions or high expectations. But not Elena Mancini. She stood up to him, challenged him, even called him out on his bedside manner and displays of inadvertent double standards.

She was bright and engaging but could be doggedly persistent. Half the hospital, including Marco's patients, were helplessly in love with her. She was sexiness and sunny disposition personified. And thanks to his own manipulations, Marco was trapped with her.

Unsettled by his constant preoccupation with the woman, he finished his fiftieth length and paused at the edge of the pool to catch his breath and admire the view of Capri as dusk approached. With any luck, if he pushed his body harder than ever before, he might fall into an exhausted, dreamless sleep.

After a moment, soft footsteps drew his attention from the sea. He turned to see Elena descending the stone steps from the terrace above. Clutching a towel, she wore a silky robe, her shapely thighs parting the opening of the gown as she walked.

Marco froze, swallowing hard. Tearing his gaze from those brief flashes of smooth-looking olive skin, he swallowed against the flood of heat engulfing him. He might be in a sauna rather than a swimming pool…

At the bottom of the steps Elena looked up, their stares locking. She blushed, hesitated as if she might turn tail and flee, one hand still on the stair rail. Marco swiftly swam across the pool and hauled his body from the water.

'I am finished,' he said, reaching for his towel and quickly rubbing it over his face and hair. 'It's all yours.' He didn't want her to feel like a guest here or to hide away or avoid him.

'Are you sure?' she said, looking uncertain, as if she was eager to be an inconspicuous visitor. 'I didn't mean to intrude. I can come back later.' Her stare briefly dipped to his chest and lower and fresh heat flared where her eyes landed so a restless rumble boiled in his gut.

Why had he put himself in this situation? The last thing he needed right now were romantic complications. He was her boss, older than her by nearly twenty years, and their fathers had fallen out professionally. But he'd insisted she marry him, dictated the stipulations, invited her to share his home, and now he had to live with the consequences. His wife was gorgeous. He wanted her. And that was not an option.

'Please. I insist,' he said, looping the towel around his neck. 'The water is lovely after the heat of the day, and the views speak for themselves.'

'Thank you.' She nodded, her expression still wary. Perhaps she could read his mind and expected him to linger or watch her swim.

Marco bit back a wave of frustration. He didn't want her grateful or uncertain. He wanted her fiery side. He wanted her to challenge him again. He wanted unreasonable things he had no right to want.

She stood awkwardly as if waiting for him to depart before she disrobed. But his feet wouldn't move.

'I wanted to say you did well today in Theatre,' he said, trying to find a topic that might lower her guard. 'You are an intuitive surgeon. You should continue with your training as soon as you are able.'

'Thank you,' she said stiffly, as if he'd offered judgement rather than praise. Obviously, she could never trust him in the slightest and he was unreasonable to expect that, having virtually blackmailed her into a loveless marriage.

'I…um…have something to suggest,' he continued, uneasy that she alone could make him falter. 'I'm attending the Innovations Symposium in Rome on Friday. I wondered if you would be interested in attending too. The programme looks excellent this year. I think it would be good for your career.'

Surprise widened her eyes and then she frowned. 'Oh… I… I had planned to be in Naples on Saturday.'

Renewed frustration tensed his body. Despite their arrangement, despite the fact that she'd promised to appear committed to this *marriage* for six months, he couldn't help the possessive twist of his insides at the idea she had a lover in Naples. One from whom she just couldn't stay away, despite her promises.

'You can still do that,' he said, impressed this time by the smoothness of his voice. 'I'm spending Friday night in a hotel so it's no problem to book two rooms. You can take the bullet train to Naples on Saturday or even fly if you prefer. You could probably catch the last train on Friday evening after the symposium if you didn't want to stay the night in Rome.'

'Okay…' She blinked rapidly as she exhaled a sigh. 'I'll…think about it.'

Marco swallowed, his throat strangely tight when he hardly ever suffered from doubt. 'I thought we might pretend it's our honeymoon.'

'Our honeymoon?' she said, her voice choked with shock, the expression doing nothing to dim the light in her lovely eyes or dispel the mocking curve of her soft lips.

Marco nodded, warming to his idea. 'We are both busy professionals. There could be no suspicion that we didn't take a longer trip. But it might look wrong if we do not mark the occasion of our marriage at all, don't you think?'

'I…'

'Don't worry,' he said, his own smile tugging at his mouth. 'I don't expect you to share my bed or even eat dinner with me, but one night in Rome won't kill you.'

Her stare narrowed as if his suggestion was a trick. 'Separate rooms?' she clarified.

'Of course.' He shrugged, uncertain why he was torturing himself this way.

It had been hard enough to sleep since she'd moved into the Caruso estate's guest house. He tossed and turned nightly, his mind plagued by guilt over her obvious doubts and disappointment from their wedding day. What young, beautiful woman imagined shackling herself to an older divorcee in such a cold, clinical and calculating way?

'I guess I could travel to visit my family on Saturday instead of Friday night,' she said and relief dragged his shoulders down a notch.

'Your family is still in Naples?' It was a question but as he pieced together the information and his former assumption was challenged, the words emerged more like a statement.

So that was who she visited every weekend. If her father's condition was serious, her regular visits made sense.

She nodded and gave another small mocking smile as her gaze swept over him. 'Do you still imagine I am visiting a lover? Is that what's bothering you?' She raised her chin, her eyes shining with mirth and challenge. 'That I'm not keeping my side of the deal?'

Was she laughing at him? Had he been jealous when he'd believed her visiting a lover? How could she deduce his motivations so effortlessly when he himself had spent days struggling to untangle them? She was tying him in knots.

But he needed to untie himself. He'd declared there was no place in this arrangement for feelings of any sort. He couldn't forget that she was a Mancini. Nor could he afford to lower his guard after Bianca's betrayal.

Marco hid his feelings with another shrug. 'I trust that we are each committed to our arrangement, so no. I'm not worried that you will renege.'

Surprisingly, his words were true. He did trust her to keep her side of the bargain. After all, apart from his wild imaginings of a lover, she hadn't given him any reason to doubt her and they would each benefit from their deception.

Elena sighed, her stare roaming the twinkling lights of Capri at night below them. 'I told you about my father's diagnosis,' she said quietly so Marco stilled, only nodding for her to continue.

'His disease has progressed rapidly,' she said, her voice betraying her pain. 'He is currently receiving end-of-life care. At Dignità Hospice, actually.' Her wary stare returned to his, a flash of defiance there.

'I see.' Marco nodded, her demands from their arrangement finally making sense as compassion rose up in him. 'I'm genuinely sorry to hear that, Elena.'

She wouldn't want his condolences; she'd proved that last time he'd offered them. But he wasn't the heartless robot she accused him of being. If only he was made that way. Then maybe he wouldn't feel so driven to honour his own beloved father in such an extreme way as to lure a beautiful woman into a fake marriage.

'How long does he have?' he asked carefully, his body still as a statue to maintain the fragile confessional.

'Weeks rather than months,' she said, looking down and rapidly blinking away the shine in her eyes.

'You are close,' Marco said, a dull ache in his belly. They had each lost something since their fathers were in partnership. He his role model and best friend and she her childhood home and Gio Mancini's professional reputation and his health.

She nodded without looking up at him. 'Papà was—*is*—a wonderful father. Supportive and loving, kind and funny.'

Marco curled his hands into fists as pain lanced through him. She might have been describing his own father. Who'd known they had so much in common?

'Despite what the media and others said—' she flicked him a hard accusing look '—he was a good surgeon. Yes, he made professional mistakes when it came to the court case and his handling of the business side of things, but he is a good man at heart. A good doctor. And this disease—' She looked down and broke off as if too choked to continue.

As if on instinct, Marco took a half step closer, his hand twitching at his side to touch her, the way he often felt with his patients when delivering their test results and the worst diagnosis possible. Now, like then, it was inappropriate. She wouldn't want his comfort. Not when *his* father had been one of those people to publicly distance himself from Gio Mancini's handling of the patient complaint. And Marco had crossed the line once before with that brief unwanted kiss on their wedding day. He couldn't touch her again, not if he ever again wanted a decent night's sleep. Because touching her might bring the return of that fire. If he touched her, held her, he might not be able to resist another kiss if she once more looked at him with that flash of desire he'd seen on their wedding day. He would want more. Want forbidden things. Sex had not been part of their bargain.

'I know what happened with Medicina dell'Apparenza is not fully to blame for his condition,' Elena continued, as if blind to Marco's restlessness, 'but he deteriorated rapidly after the stress of his bankruptcy.'

Marco nodded in understanding, rebelling against the accusation in her voice even as he acknowledged how similar they were. Each loyally devoted to family. Each grieving their patriarch's former health, strength and vitality. Each blaming the other family for what might have been, but for the professional partnership that had gone so badly wrong.

Aching to offer her some small comfort, he forced himself to keep still, stunned by how much they had in common and by the strong wave of empathy that rose up in him from nowhere, as if she'd cast him in some sort of spell.

'Stress contributes to many illnesses, as you know,' he said finally, his own grief burning in his chest. 'Some diseases are cruel and difficult to bear, both for the patient and their loved ones. I'm sorry you are going through that, on top of everything else.'

It sounded like one of his doctor speeches but in the face of her distress, his sympathy was genuine. After all, hadn't he watched his own father disappear before his eyes? Rapid weight loss no amount of Maria's delicious pasta could slow, the unbearable and uncontrolled pain of the metastases to his bones, the radiotherapy that had weakened and fatigued him further until he'd become a shell of his former self.

She watched him with a wary expression, some new fragile thread of connection between them Marco would not have believed possible before tonight. But it, just like his attraction to her, was irrelevant. Dangerous. He could not lose focus now. Not when he was so close to achieving his goals. Honouring his father. Making amends for the way his ex-wife had almost taken his family down.

Swallowing hard against the knot of grief and impotence in his chest, Marco stepped back from her and reached for his phone from the table, smoothing his features into neutrality. 'I'll leave you to your swim. Let my secretary know about the symposium.' He paused, surprised by how hard it was to walk away now that he'd seen her personal struggles. 'And…if you need to take some time off to be with your family, then do. The hospital will understand.'

CHAPTER NINE

THE INNOVATIONS SYMPOSIUM held annually in Rome was a chance for the surgical community to not only discover the latest trends and emerging research in the field, but also to network with colleagues from all over Europe. When he'd first suggested she attend, Elena had been hesitant. She was, after all, trying to avoid him whenever she could, given her determination to ignore their chemistry. But after their talk by the pool that night, after his genuine-sounding sympathy, she'd reconsidered. She had agreed to make this marriage appear real and Marco was keeping his side of the bargain.

They'd travelled to Rome together on the train that morning, each busy on their laptops. But since registering at the conference hotel, which overlooked the Colosseum, Elena had barely seen Marco. When she did catch a glimpse of him across the conference hall, he was surrounded by fellow consultants, his imposing height, good looks and dark head of hair making him easy to spot. Elena too had met several registrars. One group had invited her to join them for the evening.

Rushing from the hotel lift ten minutes past the appointed meeting time, she scanned the dimly lit bar for the group. Seeing no sign of them, she winced at the time. She'd been held up on the call to her mother. Papà had had a bad day and been confined to his bed. Her grieving mother had needed to talk to someone, not that she would hear of Elena travelling to Naples that night, insisting that she stay the night in Rome and enjoy herself for once.

Elena made her way to the bar. She would order a drink and wait ten minutes for the other registrars. If they didn't show, she'd have to assume they'd already left without her and would get an early night in order to take the first train home in the morning.

'Are you meeting someone?' a voice said as she passed.

Marco had obviously been sitting alone at a corner table, a tall glass of Peroni in front of him, but was now standing.

'Yes. No. I'm not sure, actually,' she said, flushing at how casually handsome and relaxed he looked in a sports jacket with his linen shirt open at the neck and how sometimes, when he looked at her a certain way, he made her tongue-tied. 'I was supposed to meet some other doctors that I met today, but I'm late. They might have already left without me.'

'Join me while you wait,' he said, pulling out a chair for her and signalling the waiter over to take her order.

Having also ordered a beer, Elena clasped her hands together and tried to think of something appropriate to say to her boss/fake husband. 'How did you find the symposium?' she asked, settling on an easy topic.

'Excellent. You?' He watched her intently, his unwavering gaze leaving her hot and fidgety and her mind blank.

'Very interesting,' she croaked, aware once more of that awkward chemistry between them that, rather than fading, only seemed to be growing stronger day by day. Seeing him in his swimming trunks that evening, rivulets of water coursing over his muscled body… She'd almost drooled.

'Thank you for suggesting I attend,' she added to get her mind off visions of her near-naked husband. 'I've been out of the loop for a while so it's good to understand what's happening in the field and across the rest of the world.'

She dragged in a deep breath, unable to figure Marco out any longer. Since the wedding he'd been increasingly supportive at work. He'd even been understanding about her father and suggested Elena take time off if she needed to. But she'd entered into this fake marriage with open eyes. She couldn't go around fancying her husband, imagining what it would be like to kiss him for real, to feel those strong arms hold her with passion, to sleep with him, just once… Just because she'd seen a different side to him. Sex had not been part of the negotiations.

Marco's long, capable fingers rested around his

glass as he regarded her carefully. 'Do you see yourself working in surgical oncology in the future?'

Elena hesitated. It was the first time he'd asked about her career aspirations. The topic was perfectly appropriate and professional, but the way he looked at her made her feel as if they were on a date. In fact, this entire situation—sitting with him in a bar—felt wrong. They were married but only in name. He was her boss, but they didn't get along. Their fathers had fallen out and that left them enemies of a sort.

And none of that could stop her noticing the sexy curve of his mouth as it caressed the neck of the beer bottle, the dark hair peeking from his partly unbuttoned shirt, the visions of him wet at the poolside, an impressive bulge in his trunks.

'I have an interest in endocrine surgery, actually,' she said, dragging her mind from the gutter. 'After I've re-joined my surgical training scheme and once I've passed my final fellowship exams, that's where I plan to focus.'

Marco pressed his lips together and nodded as if impressed.

'It's not easy, your work, at times, is it?' she asked, thinking of poor Signore Degano. She was also cognizant of things Marco had hinted at in the past. The emotional toll of ensuring the best patient outcomes and of breaking tragic news when even your best work wasn't enough to save someone.

'It can be a challenge,' he admitted a little stiffly, as if surprised by her observation or reluctant to admit any weakness. 'But life is full of those, isn't it? Heartbreak, loyalty to family, losing a loved one… We're all out here just trying to do our best.'

His stare lingered, his words striking multiple chords with Elena, as was his intention maybe. But again, he'd shown her another introspective side to himself in this quiet corner and for the first time she considered their families' joint past as something they had each endured. Separately but in similar ways.

'So your ex-wife did break your heart?' She was crossing a line, probing his personal life. But hadn't he done the same on their wedding day?

His mouth turned down and for a moment she thought he wouldn't answer. 'We fell out of love. That's common enough.' He shrugged. 'We had no children to consider, so I'd hoped we could divorce amicably. Bianca, unfortunately, had other ideas.'

'You said she went after your family.'

He met her stare as if surprised she'd remembered. 'She went after everything my family had built over generations. The Caruso estate, Caruso Enterprises, the family trust.' He swallowed and Elena saw his pain and shame in the way he glanced away and took another swallow of beer.

'Being betrayed by someone we once loved breaks something in us, doesn't it?' she asked softly. It was hard to admit her own humiliation, but alone here tonight with him, away from work and the estate, she felt as if the normal rules could be ignored.

'How did your ex betray you?' he asked, carefully watching her from under lowered brows.

'He's a journalist,' she said, staring at her drink where her fingernail picked at the label on the bottle. 'When the court case was hot news, when my father lost and had to file for bankruptcy and the clinic closed, he chose to write the story rather than stand by us. Stand by me. He even used information he'd only known because of our relationship.'

Marco's frown deepened. 'That's despicable. I'm sorry.'

Elena shrugged, her face hot as memories resurfaced. 'I confronted him, of course. I'd never seen him so cold as he defended his decision. He didn't even flinch when I ended it. It was as if our entire relationship had been a lie. An act.' She laughed mirthlessly. 'I know… Ironic, right, given *our* current relationship is exactly that.'

'That is not the same,' he said with a scowl, as if Rocco's actions were abhorrent to him.

'No, you're right. I was making light of it.' She smiled brightly, hoping to change the subject. 'But of course at the time I was…devastated. Heartbroken.'

Marco stared, his dark stare stormy, as if he had more he wanted to say. But in that moment they were joined by another man—tall, slightly older than Marco, with grey and balding hair.

'Dr Caruso,' the new arrival said, enthusiastically

shaking Marco's hand when he stood and offered it. 'I hoped I'd bump into you here. How are you?'

'I'm good, Leo. This is my registrar at SMC, Dr Elena Mancini. Leo Gallo is a reconstructive surgeon here in Rome.'

Elena shook the surgeon's hand, concealing a wince that he might recognise her name and recall the scandal of her father's litigation and subsequent bankruptcy, given he was a friend of Marco. But the man merely smiled and turned back to his friend.

'I heard a rumour. Is it true?' Gallo asked.

Marco frowned playfully. 'I hear plenty of rumours. What have you heard?'

Elena stared at her drink on the table, her face hot as her imagination ran wild. Had word of their marriage spread? Would she need to pretend to be madly in love with her husband in front of this man? She had told no one and Marco claimed to have only told his sister. But were people speculating about her, the way they'd done after Gio Mancini's public disgrace? Was Elena seen as the woman taking on eligible millionaire Marco Caruso, no doubt eager to get her hands on his expansive Capri estate?

'The Caruso Cancer Centre,' Leo said. 'Are you finally opening your own hospital, having talked about it for years?'

Marco smiled, his eyes shrewdly cryptic. 'Watch this space, my friend. Watch this space.' His gaze darted to Elena and Leo laughed and patted Marco's shoulder.

'Well, if you ever need a reconstructive surgeon, let me know. A little semi-retired situation on Capri might suit me down to the ground.'

'I will keep you in mind.' Marco sipped his beer, clearly unwilling to say more.

As the two men shared farewells, Elena wondered if the rumour was true. Was Marco opening his own cancer centre? She had no doubt it would succeed, as long as his head for business matched his father's. Maybe he had Dario Caruso's financial backing and the support of Caruso Enterprises.

When they were alone again, Elena watched Marco re-take his seat.

'Is it just a rumour?' she asked, glad to have another topic to discuss rather than her ex.

His expression shuttered, he made a dismissive noise in the back of his throat. Then he met her stare and sighed. 'Between you and me…?' He paused and she nodded, her heartrate accelerating that he was about to take her into his confidence. 'There will be a Caruso Cancer Centre,' he said, clearly deciding he could trust her with this. 'I am converting the main part of the estate. Renovation will begin as soon as the lawyers are done with my grandfather's will.'

Elena nodded as understanding dawned. 'So that's why you were willing to go to such drastic lengths as marrying the enemy in order to inherit?'

Now it all made sense. Marco had professional ambitions like his father and enough generational wealth to make them a reality. But he'd also needed her.

Reminding herself that they'd struck a bargain and used each other, she took a swallow of beer. His stare, when she looked up, narrowed, but not with suspicion as it had on previous occasions. His eyes seemed to peel away her layers as if he was seeing her for the first time and Elena shuddered at the intensity of it.

'Are we true enemies, you and me?' he said quietly, thoughtfully licking his lips and drawing her gaze there.

Elena felt flushed all over. He'd never looked at her that way before. She saw things in his expression she wasn't sure were real. Respect. Fascination. Desire. But did he truly find her attractive? Surely their families' past and their no-feelings arrangement made that unlikely.

Even so, excitement hijacked her breathing. What if he wanted her too? What if they could have one night together? Here in Rome away from their everyday roles and reminders…

'If we set aside our fathers' former connection,' he continued in the same contemplative voice, as if unaware of the direction of her thoughts, 'we have much in common.'

Elena dragged in a shaky breath. Was she ready to admit the extent of her attraction to him even to herself? She'd been suppressing it for so long her stomach knotted at what might happen if she were to stop—things she wanted to happen.

'Can you ever fully set aside your roots, though? she asked, clinging to the past feud to control her rush of forbidden desire. 'Who you are to the core?'

But something had shifted tonight. They'd opened up as if they might finally address what had gone wrong with their fathers' partnership, their business and their friendship. 'I will always be a Mancini and you a Caruso,' she reminded him, heart pumping. 'The past cannot be erased, no matter how much we might wish for it.'

If it could, her father might still be a plastic surgeon. He might not be terminally ill. Elena might be blissfully in love with a man she could trust. Only she didn't regret losing Rocco. She hadn't really known him. Had loved a version of him that was as fragile and deceptive as ice on the surface of a pond.

She wasn't in love with her husband. He was the enemy. But he was also direct and principled. Loyal and dependable.

'No, it cannot,' Marco agreed, reaching for his drink, his eyes still on hers.

When he said no more, when they were back at stalemate, Elena sighed, dragged her eyes from his and glanced around the bar. 'It seems my new friends have already left. I think I'll call it a night. I'm leaving on the first train. My father had a bad day today.'

For a moment, sitting opposite him, imagining possibilities, she'd been able to push the fact to the back of her mind.

Marco frowned. 'I am sorry to hear that. I'm leaving early too.' He stood. 'I will walk you upstairs.'

They left the bar together and waited for the lift in tense and awkward silence. Elena wished she'd declined his offer. Their relationship was neither one thing or another. They weren't friends, although they shared a career, a home, a past. They weren't even a regular consultant-registrar given their lingering distrust and very different personalities. They certainly weren't lovers, despite Elena's impossible fantasies and the rings they each wore.

When they were inside and with the lift to themselves, Marco added, 'Why don't you take Monday off, take some extra time to be with your family, given you attended today's symposium? It is important to cherish every moment you can.'

She frowned, something in his rigid posture and the haunted look in his eyes hinting at a vulnerability. His words from previous conversations snagged in her mind, only to dissipate as her throat tightened with unexpected gratitude. Maybe he was trying to put the past behind them.

'Thank you, Dr Caruso. I… I might do that.' She stilled, scared to move because he was still regarding her silently, his stare intense and hooded like the distrustful one of old. Only on closer inspection she saw more, saw in his eyes the same desire she felt. Was it in her imagination? And if not, should she act on it when sex, as incredible as she imagined it would be, would complicate an already complex situation?

'I think,' he said after a pause, his gaze falling to her mouth before returning, shining brighter, hotter, 'it's high time you started calling me Marco, don't you, Elena? After all, I am your husband.'

CHAPTER TEN

As the lift ascended and the seconds stretched, Marco held himself as if made of stone. Elena watched him as she considered his suggestion, her breathing speeding up. Her eyes shone with that same fire he'd come to expect every time she challenged him.

'*Fake* husband…' she said softly, those big hazel eyes blinking rapidly as if some part of her wanted to look away but could not.

'Yes,' he agreed, his body rigid with suppressed need.

He'd created this intolerable situation. He'd recklessly invited her into his life, his home, and every day had become more of a torment. Not just because of their insistent chemistry which beat at him every time they interacted, but also because he'd opened his eyes to who she really was. A smart, driven and compassionate woman, loyal to her family and their patients alike. She was no longer two-dimensional in his mind and that made her even harder to resist.

In the bar, compelled by the choices he'd made and by their shared experiences, he'd come so close to finally confiding in her about his father's death. But something had held him back. A reluctance to show this strong, caring, captivating woman the grieving, broken parts of him, the parts ugly enough to suggest a loveless marriage for material gain.

'Marco…' she whispered, as if trying out his name.

As the word left her lips, something in him snapped. With one stride, he reached her, cupping her face and tilting her chin up, their breaths mingling. He paused for a second, held in check by all the many reasons he ought to fight the urge to kiss her. She was younger than him and his professional junior. She was a Mancini and disliked him for being a Caruso. She was joy and optimism and he was jaded and distrustful and ached with grief.

'What are you waiting for?' she taunted, her pupils dilated.

When he searched her stare and saw only answering desire in the depths of her stunning green-brown eyes, he groaned aloud and covered her lips with his, finally taking what he had wanted for weeks.

Her taste, soft and sweet, flooded his body with need. The moan she released as he parted her lips and slid his tongue against hers sent a surge of triumph through him like an electric shock. When she gripped his shoulders then slid her fingers into his hair and tugged, Marco lost his mind. She wanted it too. Felt this too. Wanted him.

Marco walked her backwards until she was pressed between him and the wall of the lift, her soft curves heaven against his straining hard body.

Marco tore his mouth from hers at last, holding her face and her stare captive. 'You. You have plagued my mind since the moment we met,' he said, trying to explain the madness that had overcome him tonight. 'I wanted to kiss you the first time you challenged me that very first morning.'

Because his lips still buzzed, he traced them over her jaw to her earlobe, sucking in the scent of her skin.

'You needed challenging,' she said, tilting her head and exposing her neck as her hands slipped inside his sports jacket and around his waist, tugging his hips closer.

He couldn't bring himself to disagree. Maybe she was right. He was set in his ways. Instead, he kissed the side of her neck, inhaling deeply: lemon blossom and honey and sunshine.

'It's like an illness,' he said, his mind spinning with arousal and need and confusion. 'We made a deal. But you are a constant preoccupation. I can never relax. Not at work or at home. You are all I can think about.'

'This was all your stupid idea,' she said, panting, dropping her head back against the wall so he had better access to her neck. '*You* were the one who suggested we marry. Insisted that I move in. You should have fired me instead.'

'I should,' he said, hiding a smile.

'It's not my fault we see so much of each other,'

she continued, looking up at him with a sexy combination of lust and accusation.

Marco grunted a dismissive sound.

'This changes nothing,' she said, 'but kiss me again.' She pulled him close, making it clear she was exactly where she wanted to be.

They kissed once more. She moaned as he tilted his hips so his erection was crushed against her stomach. But still he tried to reason this away.

'I'm too old for you,' he said the next time his lips left hers, clawing back some control and hoping that voicing his objections aloud would bring them both to their senses. 'I'm your boss. *And* don't forget I'm Dario Caruso's son.'

'I don't care,' she said, chasing his lips with her own. 'I'm also legally your wife.'

Hearing her utter that word for the first time brought a surge of possessiveness to the surface. Her hands stroked his back underneath his jacket, making his blood pound harder and hotter. She licked her full, pouty bottom lip as she stared up at him and he was done for.

He crushed her close once more, capturing her lips in another searing kiss where she met fire with fire and showed him her passionate side. She moaned and pressed her body to his, her breasts to his chest, one leg hooking around his as if to hold him captive like a vine he couldn't escape, no matter how hard he struggled. But why would he want to escape?

Just then the lift pinged as it arrived at their floor. They broke apart, panting as they emerged from the fog of madness. Her dark stare held his, accusingly but also aroused. Her lips were swollen from his kisses, the delicate skin of her neck marked red from the scrape of his beard. He swallowed, trying to recall if he had ever wanted a woman so badly.

Wordlessly, they left the lift, Elena ahead of him, and marched down the corridor in the direction of their rooms. Marco dragged in some breaths, hoping to regain some composure. A battle raged inside him, guilt that he'd crossed the line with her versus his physical need for Elena Mancini.

'This is me,' he grunted, pausing outside room three-twelve. The next move must be hers. If she walked away, he would apologise for his lapse of judgement in the lift and never touch her again. After all, he'd already gone back on his word once.

She turned, her stare both bold and vulnerable. 'Invite me in,' she said, her ragged breaths audible in the quiet corridor.

Before he could sag to his knees with relief, Marco took her hand and withdrew his key card from his breast pocket, waving it in front of the sensor.

Inside his room, they silently reached for each other again, the desperation picking up where they'd left off. Elena held his face as she kissed him as deeply and frantically as he kissed her. They stumbled towards the bed, impatiently shedding clothes as they went—his jacket, her top, their shoes.

Marco's mouth dried as he took in her breasts covered by a lacy black bra and he paused to stroke her face. 'You are so beautiful.'

While he slid his hands down her bare arms which were dotted with goosebumps, she worked the buttons of his shirt. Once she'd removed it, she stroked her palms over his chest, his back, his buttocks.

'I've imagined this since that night at the pool,' she said, licking her lips, 'when I got to see most of your body.' Her hands burned his skin as impatience rattled through him.

'Then you owe me a view,' he said, holding her upper arms to drag her close so the soft mounds of her breasts pressed against his chest. 'I looked back from the top of the steps that evening but you still wore that damned robe.'

He kissed her again, need building. Her touch had ignited a fire in him, one he wasn't sure he could control. But then he hadn't been fully in control of himself since the day they'd met.

She smiled against his lips and reached for his belt and fly, opening them with hurried movements. Marco popped the clasp of her bra and sucked in an agonised breath when her perfect breasts were exposed, full and pert, their nipples peaked and rosy.

He cupped one breast in his palm, thumb brushing over the nipple, his other hand snaking around her waist to bring their naked chests flush.

'Yes,' she sighed as she stroked his erection through his trousers. 'Marco...'

He growled, chasing her lips for another deep kiss that set the roar of desire buzzing through his head. When he pulled back, his final coherent thought was one of caution and rebellion against his own body. 'Our agreement still stands.'

He needed her to be under no illusion—this was purely physical pleasure.

'Yes,' she agreed, her stare full of challenge as she ran her palms over his chest as if she couldn't quite believe she was allowed to touch. 'This is just one night. A deviation. What do they say? When in Rome...'

Despite her words, her teeth snagged her bottom lip as if she was having doubts. With excitement driving his rapid pulse, Marco pulled her lip free with the pad of his thumb, his own reservations sharpening for a second.

'Are you sure you want this? Even if it's only one night, I don't want to hurt you and we said no feelings.' Their bargain still stood.

'Yes. I want you. Let's get it out of our systems. I won't let you hurt me,' she said, sliding her fingers back into his hair, dragging him close for another deep kiss.

Relieved that she was so certain, and telling himself they each had trust issues and other priorities in their lives, Marco dragged his mouth south, capturing one nipple, stroking it with swipes of his tongue before sucking it into his mouth.

'Marco…' she cried on a sigh as he backed her down onto the bed.

He removed her jeans and underwear and then stripped off himself until they were both naked and aroused, their panting breaths evidence of their mutual desperation. They stared unashamedly at each other's bodies. She was soft curves and intriguing valleys. Olive skin and fascinating freckles. He knelt over her, prowling close to press his lips to hers until she moaned and reached for his erection. Teasing, stroking, making him forget everything outside this room. The past, the pain, the path he'd chosen. But this night would mark the end of it. The restlessness. The obsession. The weeks of secret craving. They would have their one night and move on.

His hand cupped her breast, his thumb rubbing over the nipple as they kissed. Her fingernails dug into his shoulder. He slipped his hand between her legs, stroking her in return, smiling when she moaned louder and pulled back, panting hard as she looked up at him with lust-dazed eyes.

'Does that feel good, *cara*?'

She nodded and spread her thighs another inch, her hand squeezing and tugging him in retribution.

'Do you want more?'

'Yes. I want everything. Do you have protection?'

she asked and he nodded, repositioning himself between her thighs, parting them and tracing the tip of his tongue along one inner thigh and to her centre, lapping at her until she mewled and moaned and gasped.

No more 'Dr Caruso'. Only her wild passion, her body's surrender, his name on her lips. In that moment, it didn't matter that they couldn't trust each other. They could have this. One night. Sate the madness under which he'd tried and failed to push her from his thoughts since they'd met.

He worked her with his mouth and fingers until she came, her hands gripping his hair and her broken cries calling out his name. Marco wrung every drop of pleasure from her, every moan and gasp, before locating a condom from his wash bag and re-joining her on the bed.

She reached for him as if still hungry, tugging him down on top of her, kissing her taste from his lips as she parted her thighs to cradle his hips.

He gripped one thigh in his hand, raising it over his hip as he nudged inside her, his own groan of pleasure trapped in his chest at her tight warmth.

'Yes,' she whispered, holding his stare, sliding her fingers into his hair as she crossed her ankles in the small of his back. 'Yes.'

They moved together, their bodies perfectly attuned as if made for each other. She clung to him, her hands on his shoulders, his arms, his back. Marco forgot to hold a part of himself back, forgot who they were, forgot their pasts. There was only this. Him. Her. Pleasure.

'Elena—' he said as he thrust harder, faster, giving himself over to the moment and the need for this woman that had steadily built day by day.

Elena came again, crying out his name as she held him tight. Marco let go, finding his own euphoric release. It was only as the high dwindled and he caught his breath that some logical part of his brain presented a reality check. It would have to suffice. He had nothing to offer his wife but this one night. But if he was brutally honest, he already knew that it wasn't going to be enough.

CHAPTER ELEVEN

On the Tuesday after the symposium in Rome, Elena's first priority when she returned to work was to visit Fredo Degano, who was still a patient on the high dependency unit. His pancreatic fistula had delayed his reintroduction to solid food and complicated his post-op recovery. The internal haemorrhage had necessitated a blood transfusion and iron supplements. And today, the nurses reported a new worrying development.

'Signore Degano,' she said, offering the lovely old man a smile. 'How are you feeling? The nurses tell me you've been coughing quite a bit.'

'Not too bad, Dr Mancini,' he said, clearly far from well.

Elena hid her frown of concern and reached for his pulse, continuing to perform a full examination of his cardiac and respiratory systems and his abdomen. When she had finished, she perched on the edge of his bed.

'I'm worried that you have a chest infection,' she said softly. 'They are quite common after surgery and with a prolonged period of inactivity. I'm going to order a chest X-ray and run some more blood tests. Are you coughing anything up?'

Degano nodded weakly. 'A little.'

'I'm going to start you on some different antibiotics and ask the physiotherapist to see you again,' Elena said. 'Try and squash this thing before it takes hold, okay?'

The patient tapped the back of her hand affectionately in response.

'Would you like me to call your wife to explain what's happening?' Elena asked, compassion for him welling up.

'Yes, please. She worries.'

'Of course she does. She loves you.' That was what marriage was all about. In sickness and in health. At least real marriages were anyway…

At the desk in the ward office, Elena ordered the urgent X-ray and prescribed more antibiotics, preoccupied by her concerns. But at least they stopped her thinking about Marco, the night in Rome, the situation in which she'd put herself. Sleeping with her fake husband. Disloyally wanting Dario Caruso's son. Falling completely apart in his arms as she'd surrendered to pleasure so much greater than she'd imagined. How would she face him and act normal when she'd replayed every moment of that night over and over ever since?

She'd just completed her referral to the physiotherapist when a shadow fell over the doorway.

Marco stood there, his expression carefully blank but his eyes shining with memories of what they'd done that night. 'Dr Mancini. How are you today?'

Elena's pulse flew. She hadn't seen him since creeping from his hotel room before dawn on Saturday. He'd been gorgeously relaxed in sleep, his hair dishevelled, dark stubble on his face, the sheet around his lean hips. And seeing him now, recalling how it had felt to be so utterly consumed by him, she realised with a sinking stomach that she wanted him still.

'I'm well, Dr Caruso.' Her body heated as she held his stare, memories of the passionate events of that night threatening to make her blush. His question was perfectly polite and professional, but now that she'd heard that deep voice groan her name, it was easy to hear the subtext. He wanted to know if she had any regrets over sleeping with him. She had heaps, but only because she couldn't wipe that night from her mind. 'And yourself?'

After the first time, they'd showered together. She'd gone down on him under the spray, torturing him with pleasure as he'd muttered broken curses and watched her mouth like a starving man. Back in the bedroom, he'd returned the favour, returned the torture before they'd used his second condom and then finally, his third and last.

Marco nodded, his eyes seeming to see beneath her clothes as he stepped inside the room and lowered his voice. 'You left.'

He didn't sound angry or even disappointed, just matter-of-fact, which was somehow worse. Because the minute she'd quietly sneaked from his hotel room and their one night had officially ended, she'd wanted to turn back, wanted to change the rules and keep the fantasy that their connection was real, alive for a while longer. But it was just sex. And now they were back to reality.

'I wanted to catch the early train to Naples, and I didn't want to wake you.' Elena looked past him towards the nurses' station in case anyone might overhear, desperate to keep what had transpired between just them and not the rest of the hospital.

By sneaking out that morning without saying goodbye, she'd given herself time to try and come to terms with what she'd done. Time she'd needed to remind herself of all the reasons it could never happen again. He was still his father's son. She didn't want a real relationship. And they'd agreed to one night.

'We missed you at work yesterday,' he said, causing Elena's pulse to double excitedly. Had he missed her? Been thinking about her? Like her, craving another night?

'We were very busy here,' he qualified, and she nodded, defeated, her heart surging with panic. Of course he'd only missed her because of the workload at the hospital. Whereas she was all over the place.

'How is your father?' Marco asked, his professional persona back in place as if they might be discussing a patient.

'He is as well as can be expected, thank you,' she said, both confused by and expecting his distance.

On Friday night he'd been just a man—passionate, aroused, desperate for Elena despite all his reservations. Despite how them sleeping together had complicated an already complex situation.

She held in a sigh of regret. Obviously, sleeping with him had been a big mistake.

'I think it raised his spirits to see me,' she finished, desperate to think about anything other than how she still wanted this man who didn't want her.

'I'm sure it did.' Marco paused as if he might say more. His gaze shifted over her face, to her lips and back. Elena held her breath. Tried not to overinterpret anything from his stare.

'I'm glad you are here,' she said, trying to break the unbearable tension and to distract her thoughts away from the forbidden: her husband. 'I was going to call you. I think Signore Degano has a chest infection. I've ordered some tests and prescribed antibiotics. I was just about to call his wife, unless you wish to do so.'

'No. You can call her,' he said with a frown of concern. 'I came to review him myself before my new patient clinic this afternoon. He is not progressing as smoothly as I would like.' His frown persisted and Elena wondered if perfectionist Marco took every patient setback personally. The work of doctors often traversed a tightrope between doing good and spawning complications.

'No.' She sighed. 'I'm worried too.' She waited. Part of her expected him to be guarded with her. If he possessed doubts of accountability with regard to Signore Degano's post-operative complications, Elena would be the last person in whom he would confide. Even after their night in Rome.

'Carry on, then,' he said, casting her one final cool glance. 'I'll review him myself to confirm your findings.'

Elena watched him walk away with another sigh. She could have predicted that he would double-check; that was Marco's way. Maybe after that night, after they'd trusted each other enough to be intimate, a small part of her had hoped things might be…different between them. That they might open up more. Trust each other more. Finally lay the past to rest. But just because they'd called a brief truce in order to consummate their fake marriage didn't mean they meant anything more to each other than strangers who worked together.

If, now that she'd slept with her husband, it stung to know he still couldn't trust her fully, not even at work, that was on her. After all, with the exception of their bargain, he'd made her no promises.

Days later, Elena returned to the estate guest house after work to another stunning Mediterranean evening. She showered, ate the gnocchi Maria had left in the fridge and took her book and a chilled glass of Soave to the terrace to watch the sun set.

With both the view and Marco as a distraction, Elena barely made it through a page before she abandoned the book. But she would not think of him. She inhaled, listened to the bees hum and the birds sing their evening song. But it wasn't long before she wondered where Marco was at that moment. Was he thinking about her? Did he wake at night searching the bed for her as she did for him? Was there any part of him that yearned for more than one night of passion? Or was he firmly back in control of himself, leaving her alone to ponder that, if not for the past, for their trust issues, if they'd met in a parallel universe, they might have a shot at a real relationship?

Elena sighed and sipped her wine, her mind returning to Rocco's betrayal. Since, she'd told herself she was too focused on caring for her father to date. But in reality, she was scared to expose her feelings again and be hurt.

Trust was intangible. A mirage. It appeared solid enough, but its true reliability only came after many tests and with the passage of time. And with her energies fixed on work and family, putting her heart on the line again had been a low priority. But the way she'd felt that night in Rome with Marco made her wonder if she might be ready to reshuffle her priorities a little. To think about dating again soon. To meet a person she was sure about, one who wanted her just as she was and did not care that she was Gio Mancini's daughter.

When Enzo appeared, trundling past on his estate buggy, Elena was grateful for the interruption and waved.

'*Buonasera*, Elena,' he said.

'*Buonasera*,' she called, coming to her feet. 'Please tell Maria thank you for the gnocchi. It was delicious.'

'I will,' he said, smiling as he brought the buggy to a complete stop. 'My wife is so used to cooking for a large family. She always makes too much for just the three of us. She is constantly foisting food onto people.'

Elena smiled. 'She will be glad when the rest of the Carusos return to Capri, I'm sure. Do they have plans to spend any time here this summer?'

With just her and Marco and Enzo and Maria, the estate felt too big. Marco had been correct when he'd assured her that she would have her privacy. And she only had two more weeks of her locum position to go before she would leave Capri, maybe for good. At the idea of never seeing Marco again, her stomach pinched.

'I don't think so.' Enzo's expression saddened. 'Allegra and Ginevra struggle to be here since Dario died, but hopefully as the grief eases they will return. The family love this place. So many happy memories.'

Elena froze, her smile sliding from her face. Dario Caruso was dead? How had she not heard that news? Why hadn't Marco said anything? He too must be grief-stricken. But of course he would not confide in her, a Mancini. A woman not to be trusted.

'Marco's father died?' she said aloud, stunned, her mind racing over all her conversations with Marco. Every accusation she'd cruelly hurled. Every comparison and assumption she'd made about him and his family. Pain griped in her stomach. She'd wrongly thought the Mancinis were the only ones suffering after the Medicina dell'Apparenza scandal. But why hadn't Marco said anything? Why keep it a secret rather than set the record straight? Was his distrust of her so great even now? His emotional guard so impenetrable she had no hope of ever being let in?

Sensing her shock and perhaps feeling it wasn't his place to discuss it further, Enzo nodded then hastily bid her a lovely evening and set off for his villa.

Elena stared blindly at the stunning view, her head full of regrets and confusion and frustration. She'd thought she was beginning to see the real Marco, something that had convinced her to sleep with him despite the risk that she might want more than one night. But in reality, he'd kept her at arm's length.

Now it was obvious that, despite them working together all these weeks, despite them sleeping together, his distrust for her matched or maybe even surpassed hers for him. Reminded of the pain of Rocco's betrayal, humiliation and confusion swirled inside her. She slipped her feet into her ballet flats and set off in search of Marco. She wanted to understand what had happened to Dario. To confront Marco for his secrecy. To understand his feelings on the loss and offer condolences and be there for him. Not that he would need or want that from her of all people.

After frantically checking the pool and the gym, she reached his villa and spied an open set of French windows, pale linen curtains billowing in the light evening breeze.

'Hello,' she called, tapping the open door before stepping inside a beautiful but empty living room. She crossed to a tiled hallway and glanced left and right. 'Hello?'

Catching the sound of the creak of leather, she turned in that direction towards another open door. It was a library or study and Marco sat behind a large mahogany desk, headphones on and his back to her as he faced the ocean view from the windows.

Freezing in the doorway, Elena's heart clenched. He looked lost. Alone. Or maybe she was imagining things because she'd foolishly thought she knew him after just one meaningless night in his arms.

Except for her it hadn't been totally meaningless, and that was what stung the most now.

Not wanting to startle him, she tapped on the door to draw his attention. He turned, surprise raising his eyebrows as he removed the headphones and paused the music she heard coming from them.

'Elena, is everything okay?' He stood, his worried gaze sweeping over her from head to toe.

'I'm fine,' she said and his stare turned heated with a glow of desire he'd kept better hidden while at work.

Elena stepped into the room, her breathing tight because she didn't know where to begin and had so many feelings, all of which were forbidden. 'Your father died?' she blurted, wincing when his expression hardened as he stepped around his desk. Part of her wanted to touch him, to comfort him, but that was no longer allowed. Nor could she risk it, not when her physical need for him was barely contained by her anger that he'd misled her.

'Yes,' he stated simply. Clearly, he didn't want to talk about it, maybe the reason he'd kept it secret.

'When?' she asked in a whisper, the part of her that was stupidly hurt that he hadn't trusted her with the news curling inwards.

This reminded her of their first meeting, when discord and distrust had tainted their working relationship.

'Six months after Medicina dell'Apparenza closed,' he said, his voice flat and unemotional.

Elena sighed with frustration. They weren't discussing a surgical technique. This was his father.

'I'm sorry. I didn't know.' She stepped closer, drawn to the pain in his dark eyes. Drawn to comfort. To help. Even if he couldn't trust her.

'How did you find out?' he asked, his frown deepening as if with anger.

'Enzo let it slip, but it was my fault,' she rushed on. 'I asked him when your family might return to the estate.'

Marco's eyes narrowed with suspicion. 'He is not in trouble. There is no need to defend him. I am not the vengeful tyrant you might have coloured me in your imaginings.'

'Of course… I know you are not.' Elena flushed, confused by how little she actually knew this man, despite weeks of working for him and that incredible night in Rome.

'I grew up with Enzo and Maria,' he said. 'They are like a second set of parents to me.'

'Why didn't you tell me about your father?' she begged. Hadn't they begun to trust each other a little since then? At least professionally. Enough to sleep together. Or maybe the trust was one-sided… 'I told you about my father, his bankruptcy, his Parkinson's.'

He stepped closer still, prowling her way, his expression darkly intent and heartbreakingly vulnerable at the same time. 'It's like you said. I am a Caruso and you a Mancini. You accused me of being…what was it now?…"arrogant and ruthless and cold". Yes, I think that covers it. Maybe I assumed that, given your opinion of me, you would be uninterested in what had befallen my father after the court case.'

Now that she'd learned this information, Marco's pain and grief were obvious in the haunted expression in his eyes and the lines around his mouth. The many things he'd said about loss finally made sense. How could she have been so self-absorbed as to miss those clues before?

'Well, you're wrong,' she said, her breaths speeding up as indignation flared. 'I *am* interested. I *do* care, so why don't you tell me now?'

'Very well,' he said, pausing before her, his emotions carefully concealed, as they often were. He wore the same stoic expression at work when delivering bad news to a patient or family member. But now that she knew him better, she saw it for the mask it was. Because of course he cared. He cared deeply. Passionately. With every part of himself.

'He died of metastatic stomach cancer,' Marco continued, and Elena gasped with shock. 'He left his family bereft, his business interests to my younger sister and the Caruso estate, which should have been his, mine to inherit instead.'

'I'm so sorry,' she repeated, because nothing else seemed appropriate. 'That's why you want to build the Caruso Cancer Centre here? For your father?' Marco would absolutely detest that the disease that had taken his father's life was the one for which Marco treated his own patients.

'It was his dream too.' Marco shrugged but the flare in his eyes told her she'd guessed correctly. 'It is the very least I can do.'

'What do you mean?'

'I am his son.' He swallowed, as if desperately trying to claw back control when she would have him lose it and reach for her for comfort. 'A surgical oncologist. I should have been able to help him somehow. But it was too late.'

'You couldn't treat your own father,' she pointed out and then winced because he already knew that.

'Of course not.' His swallow seemed pained. 'But at least when I have full legal possession of the property, I can finish our joint dream and build him a legacy fitting for the good, hard-working doctor he was.'

Elena nodded, her own feelings so conflicted her throat ached with sadness for all both families had lost in the past few years.

Then a chill spread through her as another thought occurred. 'Do you blame me for his death because I'm a Mancini?' she asked, her pulse throbbing like thunder as she tried to be brave in anticipation of his answer. 'Do you blame my father for what happened to yours?' He'd talked about stress contributing to disease. And given she'd initially blamed him and his family for her father's diagnosis, she couldn't blame him if he did. Only part of her wanted her and Marco to somehow absolve each other for the past.

For a second, he glanced away. Elena's stomach twisted. Of course he blamed Gio Mancini. For his lapse of judgement over the civil law case. Just like she'd blamed Dario Caruso for betraying her father's friendship.

Only now that she knew this man better, her anger and resentment was no longer enough to keep her warm.

When his stare returned to hers, she saw he had hidden any trace of vulnerability behind that detached mask. 'We will never know how much the stress of what happened contributed to each of our fathers' illnesses.'

'No, we won't,' she conceded, blinking against the sting of unshed tears. The divide between her and Marco, rather than closing as she'd hoped after Rome, seemed to be widening.

'Then why don't we leave it there?' he said.

But she couldn't leave things like this. 'I know there is hurt and blame and accusation on both sides…' Shame for her ignorance and unfair accusations washed over her as she stepped closer. 'Both our families have lost so much. But you could have trusted me with this sooner. Instead, you let me talk about my father, about the bankruptcy and the scandal, as if we were the only ones suffering. When that obviously wasn't the case.'

Marco pressed his lips together then said, 'Life is never that straightforward or one-sided.'

She nodded. 'I… I don't know what to say beyond I'm so sorry, Marco. I know I am nothing to you. The last person in whom you could confide…' She paused, some foolish part of her hoping he might argue. 'I know we can never be friends, that we are not a proper married couple, that you don't trust me in the slightest,' she continued, 'but if you ever want to talk about what happened, I want you to know that I will listen. Without judgement or blame or name-calling. I promise.'

She looked down, her eyes stinging because she too would soon know the grief of losing her father. How much she and this proud, caring man she'd once thought a stranger had in common…

'You once said that words are just words,' he said quietly. 'It is actions that speak the truth.'

She nodded, surprised that he'd remembered. 'That's what I'm saying now. We do not need to be enemies,' she whispered, her hands twitching to touch him, hold him, to feel as close to him as when he'd held her in his arms. 'We are a loyal son and daughter, that's all. It was never our fight.'

'We are not enemies,' he said, his jaw clenched as his stare dipped to her mouth, as if either dreading what she might say next or eager to silence her with a kiss. But maybe it was just Elena hung up on their apparent connection that night. Maybe Marco no longer craved her the way he had seemed to in Rome. Maybe for him, it was done.

'I want to help somehow…' she pleaded, hoping he would lower his guard and let her in emotionally.

'I want to turn back time,' he said sadly, and her heart cracked open because she felt the same. She would give anything to have more time with her father.

He did not need to add that they couldn't always have what they wanted. She heard it anyway.

Rather than dismiss her or step away, he stood frozen before her, tension a pulsing forcefield between their bodies.

'Maybe you should go,' he said, his voice a challenge as if he expected her to abandon him in his hour of need, maybe as his ex-wife had done. She must have filed for divorce during that horrible time when Dario Caruso was battling cancer. He'd told her as much the day of their wedding when she'd been too caught up in her own feelings to notice or probe.

She should leave. Give him space. Retreat and analyse what she had learned and what it meant for how she felt about him. But he had consoled her over her father, supported her these past weeks, giving her permission to take time off to be with her family. She would not see him suffer alone without a fight.

'I… I need to know you are okay, Marco,' she said, her chest rising with every rapid breath as she stepped closer still.

He stiffened as if fearful of her touch. 'I am fine. I have a goal. Inherit and build the clinic. As I promised him. Once that is achieved, I can finally lay my father to rest and move on.'

'And what if building the clinic in his name

doesn't help fill the void?' she pressed. She understood him now because she too faced her father's mortality. She already grieved the Gio Mancini he had once been. That grief would only continue when he passed. But nothing, not even a sense of having redressed the past with her naive deal with her fake husband, would take away the pain.

Marco's growing and immovable frown did nothing to stop her from inching closer still. 'You once said I did not know you,' she whispered. 'But that is no longer true. I know this part of you, because we are the same. We both grieve our fathers. We each hope that salvaging something from their soured partnership will help to ease our grief, to make amends for what was lost. But what if we are wrong? What if the best way to honour our fathers is to forgive? Be the best surgeons we can be, like they were. To live our own lives as fully and happily as they did.'

'Stop,' he said, his voice dangerously low, his breaths laboured.

But she could not. Her stubborn streak prevailed. 'I'm sorry for the horrible things I said. For the hurtful and ignorant accusations. You are a good man, Marco. A good surgeon. Just like your father. It's no excuse, but I lashed out because I'm hurting. Watching Papà fade, the way you had to watch Dario, is agony. I don't need to tell you because I see it in your eyes.'

With a groan of frustration, he reached for her,

tugging her into his arms. He held her to his chest, where his heart thundered against her cheek. 'It will be okay,' he whispered into her hair. 'You will get through this. You are strong, the way he raised you.'

Fighting tears for them both, Elena held him back, her arms around his waist. But the comfort was short-lived. He pushed at her shoulders and eased her back, dropping his hands to his sides.

'Go,' he said, something pleading in his voice even as his stare burned with need.

Elena shook her head. There was anguish and vulnerability in his expression, but also desire. The one thing she'd secretly hoped to see because she felt it too. This wasn't over. One night had not diminished the craving at all, only made it worse.

Desperate to soothe both his turmoil and her own, Elena surged onto the balls of her feet and kissed him. For a second, he stood unmoving. But a second later, he groaned. His arms crushed her close, his lips moving against hers as he commanded and deepened the kiss that somehow felt like coming home.

'We said we wouldn't do this,' he panted against her lips, as his fingers slid into her hair and he tilted her face back and ravaged her neck with his lips and the scrape of his facial hair. 'We said one night.'

Elena sagged against his hard body with relief. 'I know…' she replied, her own hands roaming his arms and shoulders, pressing him close. She cupped his face and they stared into each other's eyes. His were stormy and conflicted, glowing with pain and desire and confusion.

'I can't stop thinking about you,' she said. 'About Rome…' And how that one night had changed everything.

She didn't want to hate him. She wanted to find their common ground. To work their way out of their families' past together. She'd already lost one significant relationship because of this scandal. She didn't want the rest of her life and her future relationships to be defined by bitterness and regret. It was time to let it go and to try and be happy and fulfilled.

'We promised.' He kissed her again, as if snatching the opportunity before they came to their senses and upheld their agreement. But Elena didn't want to wake up. She wanted to burn up in his arms.

'They are just words,' she reminded him, sliding a hand between them to stroke the erection straining the front of his linen trousers. Marco swallowed a choked sound of pleasure, as he palmed her breast and stroked his thumb over the nipple as if he couldn't stop himself from touching her. Then, sliding a hand under her dress and between her thighs, he kissed her with thrilling force that she returned, her tongue matching his stroke for stroke. They were two passionate souls, she and Marco. In his arms she felt alive. Close wasn't close enough. It might never be.

Breaking free from their kiss, Marco picked her

up and deposited her on the edge of the massive wooden desk. 'Why wouldn't you leave?' he asked, delicately stroking his fingers down the side of her face and neck as if she were an exquisite work of art he needed to touch to make sure it was real.

'I couldn't,' she said. 'I want you.' She wanted him to lean on her. To open up to her. To show her this final side of himself, the one just as stuck in the past as she had been.

He peeled down the shoulder of her dress and bra, cupping her breast and sucking her nipple. He slid his hand inside her underwear to stroke her. Then pulled back to watch her, transfixed by her pleasure as his fingers probed and stroked and plunged inside her.

'Marco…' she moaned. Gripping his hips in one hand and the back of his neck with the other, she tugged his mouth back to hers, kissing him deeply, wildly, as pleasure infected her entire body. The high built and built as they each lost control.

'Elena…' he groaned, stroking her faster as he wrapped one arm around her hips.

She reached for his fly. Shoved his trousers and underwear down and took his erection in her hand, tugging at him until he stopped touching her long enough to peel down her underwear.

'Marco…' she cried, dropping her head back on a moan as he once more sucked her nipple. 'I need you, now.'

She pulled him closer, wrapped her legs around

his hips, leaned back on one elbow and tugged him down on top of her.

'Yes!' she cried as his erection nudged her clit and their kisses grew wilder. Desperate. Denial abandoned.

'No condom,' he muttered against her lips, his kisses unrelenting as his fingers tweaked her nipple and she hovered close to climax. But it wasn't enough.

'Don't care,' she said. 'Don't need it. On the pill.' She was on fire, the likes of which she had never known. Even the three times they'd had sex in Rome couldn't compare to this, because she knew him now. Knew what he battled. What he held back. And she wanted every unguarded part of him.

At his agonised groan of surrender, she pushed her tongue against his and held him captive as he sank inside her, clutching her tight in return. They panted, breathing each other's air. Caressed each other's face as they stared.

Perfection. There was no other word to describe the way he made her feel. Safe and protected. Seen and understood. Alive and on fire.

'Don't stop,' she said as he held her flush to his chest.

His hips thrust and she crossed her ankles, wrapped around him as if she might never let go. He powered into her so the desk rattled under the force. But every stroke was honest and passionate.

Open and desperate. Needing release and each other the way they needed air.

'Elena…' he groaned, rearing back to stare down at her as he held her against his bucking hips.

'Yes, yes…' she cried, her orgasm stealing her voice so all she could do was cling to him and hold him as he too groaned through the storm of pleasure that seemed to last an age.

Elena slid her fingers through his hair as their hearts slowed, side by side. As they caught their breath, he stiffened, coming out of the daze first.

Elena released him, sensing his emotional withdrawal even before he'd stepped away. He helped her down from the desk and retrieved her underwear from the floor and handed it over.

'We cannot do this again,' he said with a frown that sent her seeing red. He rebuttoned his trousers and shoved his hands in his pockets.

'Don't—' she bit back. 'Don't do that.' Her voice was pleading but she didn't want him to retreat behind that controlled, driven mask he wore.

'We agreed there would be no complications to our arrangement,' he said, all but breaking her heart. 'That was…stupid. I don't want you to be hurt when the time comes for us to divorce.'

Crushed by pain, Elena stooped to slide on her underwear, the abrupt change in him turning her stomach. For a moment there, she'd felt closer to him than ever. Felt that they had finally found a common thread on which they might build. That if only they could learn to trust each other, they might have a chance at a real relationship. But, in spite of everything, Marco still seemed reluctant to be completely open with her.

'Fine,' she said, impressed with the clarity of her voice when all she could taste was rejection. 'It won't happen again.' She brushed past him and headed for the door.

He gripped her arm, stalling her, his stare pleading. 'I am consumed with the pending inheritance and the Caruso Cancer Centre. I promised my father before he died that I *would* build our dream. I owe him so much. He helped me.' Something in his voice was desperate, calling to her even now. 'I have to put that first, above *everything.* I have to think of my family. There isn't enough of me left to love you or anyone else right now.'

She nodded, hating that he'd warned her who he was the day of their wedding when he'd told her about his first wife, and then again before they'd slept together in Rome.

'I never asked you to love me,' she said. But his rejection raised the demons her ex had spawned. Because, just like Rocco, of course he could never love Gio Mancini's daughter.

His frown deepened, his regret no compensation at all. 'I…we both have trust issues. I don't have time to work through mine at the moment. I thought you understood.'

Another shard of pain lanced her. 'Don't worry,

Marco,' she croaked, trying to be brave. 'We do understand each other. We always have.'

Then she turned and walked out, her resolve building with each step. She would hold it together for the duration of her locum position, leave Capri as planned and squash any feelings she might have for her husband. She might be able to trust him to a degree, but it was clear that with him unwilling to let go of the past, unwilling to let her in and see her for who she was, she'd never be able to trust him with her battered heart.

CHAPTER TWELVE

THE DAY AFTER Elena had discovered the news of his father's passing, the day after he'd broken his promise that their physical relationship was over, Marco called his sister Ginevra in Rome.

'*Ciao, come stai?*' his sister asked, that hint of sadness that had been there since they'd lost their father still in her voice.

'I'm well, and you?' He spun his chair to face the view from his office at SMC, his vision drifting out of focus.

He was still stunned by his physical weakness for his wife. She'd walked into his home office last night with fire in her eyes and he'd instantly known he would lose his internal battle to resist her, the same battle that had endlessly raged since he'd awoken in Rome to find her side of the bed empty. When she'd shown him her compassion and concern and while gently encouraging him to open up, his doubts had grown and multiplied. When he'd held her and comforted her in her moment of grief for Gio's looming mortality, he'd known he was done for. He'd selfishly leaned on her, sucking comfort from their simmering passion to block out the pain she'd opened up with her gentle words and sympathetic looks.

'All good here,' Gin said, meaning that their mother was fine. Still grieving Dario, but bravely getting on with life. 'What's up?'

Marco held in a sigh, his mind still scattered because, despite what he'd said to her the night before, he was equally consumed by his wife. But he needed to get his priorities back on track. 'I wanted to know how my purchase of the Dignità shares is progressing.'

After last night, after his monumental lapse, he needed to start tying up loose ends. Elena's locum position was coming to an end. She would then return to her life in Naples, their 'separation' the start of the apparent demise of their marriage. He wanted her to have the handover documentation, to keep his side of the bargain before she left.

'These things take time,' Ginevra said, her voice full of amusement. 'Even for a beloved brother. Why?'

Marco took a deep breath, determined to keep it all together. If he could stop being intimate with his wife, he could once more focus on their agreement. Because last night she'd raised so many doubts in him he felt as if he was losing his mind and his grip on his entire life.

Who was he without his goals? He'd spent most of his adult life honing his skills as a surgeon and at least the past few years building a dream of his own hospital, a dream sanctioned and encouraged by Dario. But what if Elena was right? What if his plan to honour his father didn't bring closure or an easing of his grief? Where would that leave him?

'No reason. I—' He dragged in a breath, unable to articulate one tenth of his feelings. Because every single one of them led back to Elena somehow. 'Just putting things in order.'

'Has fake married life already lost its lustre?' Gin asked quietly and without judgement, although she'd been quick to point out the multiple flaws in his brilliant plan to outwit the archaic inheritance clause in his grandfather's will. Marrying without love seemed an insanity to his romantic sister. Marrying Gio Mancini's daughter… Well, that had baffled her into a rare silence.

'You do not need to worry about me, sister,' Marco said, refusing to analyse his *marriage;* it wasn't real. It would soon be over. Away from the constant, unrelenting temptation of her, his perspective would return. Then he'd be free to give all his energy to building the Caruso Cancer Centre in remembrance of Dario. It was the right thing to do.

'What is she like, this Mancini woman?' Gin asked.

Marco searched his mind for a concise descriptor of Elena, unable to settle on just one. 'Smart, beautiful, fun,' he replied without thinking. 'I'm sure you two would get along if you were ever to meet.' But there would be no need for that. Unlike their marriage, their divorce could be wholly managed by the lawyers.

He should feel relieved that all his dreams would soon be in his grasp. But the idea of never seeing Elena again… A hollow feeling slipped under his guard, one he brushed aside.

'Ah…so she has an outspoken side,' Gin said, her voice full of amusement. 'I bet that's been interesting.'

Marco made a non-committal sound. Interesting, invigorating, arousing… And ensuring he lost endless hours of sleep.

'Marco…' Ginevra said suspiciously. 'Are you and your wife…consummating your marriage, by any chance? Is that a good idea, given you expect this woman to divorce you in a few months?'

Marco swallowed. Consummating? It felt more destructive than that, as if his life would never be the same after her. She was changing him, his wife. Forcing him to see himself as others might. Forcing him to be more open. But he couldn't think about that now.

'I won't be discussing my sex life with my little sister,' Marco warned, adding a rarely used firmness to his voice.

'Fine. I don't mean to pry.' Ginevra sighed, turning serious. 'But I care about you. I know how your last divorce cut you up, how Bianca hurt you at your lowest point.'

'This time is different,' he said. 'The divorce settlement is pre-arranged. And sadly, Papà is not here to bail me out.'

'I worry about you being alone,' Gin continued. 'It's not healthy. You are in your prime. Successful. Wealthy. Still handsome.'

'Such praise,' he teased, then became serious. 'I cannot think about any of that now. About myself. I have a plan, one I'm so close to achieving. Maybe once the cancer centre is up and running I'll have capacity to think about my private life… But I need to do this, Gin. We all loved him, but I am the only doctor in the family. You know it all but killed me to be unable to help him, especially when it's my job to treat people with cancer.'

'Of course. I understand. Although it wasn't your job to be his doctor.'

Marco clenched his jaw. Elena had said the same the night before. 'I know. But I still feel responsible. Guilty. He helped me settle things financially with Bianca, encouraged me to swiftly divorce rather than dragging it out for years. And he was right. None of us could have predicted how little time he had left. But had my divorce become another prolonged legal battle, I might have been more distracted in his final months.' And he might have found forgiving himself even harder.

There was no one more regretful of his past than Marco. He'd brought Bianca into the family. He'd made a mistake in loving her, and she'd gone after an unreasonable divorce settlement when his father was sick and the entire family was reeling.

'I need to pay him back somehow,' Marco added, guilt a foul taste in his mouth. 'To future-proof the Caruso family for you and Mamma.'

'Papà would just want us all to be happy,' Gin said quietly. 'You know that was his final wish.'

'I am content. I will be more so when the cancer centre opens its doors to the first patients. I promised him I would finish it.'

'*Va bene*,' Gin said in defeat. 'Just be careful with your wife. I don't want you to get hurt again.'

Marco winced, his current predicament—craving his wife but trying to ignore it—felt pretty painful. Agonising. 'This time everything is in writing, so there's no chance of a repeat of the Bianca situation.' Plus, he didn't love Elena. He'd been careful to keep feelings out of it. He didn't want either of them to be hurt.

Gin paused, her silence a warning sound. 'I wasn't talking about property or assets, Marco. I'm talking about your heart, your feelings. Just...take care, *sì*.'

'Of course. Let me know as soon as Dignità is mine. *Ciao*.' He rang off, his unfocused stare still on the view.

The best way to ensure that he didn't get hurt again, to make sure he didn't hurt Elena, was to continue to keep feelings out of his marriage. That meant no more touching his wife. No more sex. And for good measure, he would keep personal conversations to a minimum. Because if he let her all the way in, she might see that he was broken. In order to finish what he'd started, he needed to be strong. And feelings… They just made him weak.

Elena hadn't seen Marco since that night in his study at the estate. The distance, combined with a visit to Naples at the weekend, had cleared her head and hardened her heart. She would not allow herself to make another painful mistake, to develop feelings for a man who could not return them, like Rocco. She understood Marco because they were both grieving. But he wanted to fix his pain by shutting down his emotions and literally building a 'monument' to his father. Whereas Elena just wanted to live in the moment, spend time with those she loved and, one day, find someone she could share the rest of her life with.

On Monday morning, Elena walked onto ICU, where Signore Degano had been admitted over the weekend. What had begun as a post-op chest infection had, over the weekend, rapidly deteriorated into a left lower lobe pneumonia and moderate hypoxic respiratory failure, a concerning setback.

Elena finished reviewed the patient's notes, learning he was being treated with non-invasive ventilation or continuous positive airway pressure, CPAP for short. She left the office and made her way to

Fredo's bed, when she spied Marco already sitting at the bedside in a hard plastic chair.

Elena froze, mesmerised by his quiet solitude. He sat unmoving and seemingly lost in thought. Signore Degano appeared to be asleep, the CPAP mask covering his face.

As she hesitated, her pulse flew, her heart a dull throb in her chest. Was Marco, like her, very concerned for their patient's post-operative recovery? Was he pointlessly blaming himself for the unforeseen complications of Fredo's surgery? Or maybe he was thinking about his own father. He must have spent many an hour sitting at Dario's bedside, wondering which visit might be the last time he saw his father alive.

Pain squeezed her insides—pain she tried not to feel in case it weakened her resolve. He'd kept secrets from her, rejected her compassion, rejected *her*. But seeing him this way, Elena realised once more how wrong she'd been about Marco. He felt things deeply. Was compelled to act with integrity, setting high standards for himself both professionally and in his personal life. He carried so much responsibility—for his patients, his family, his father. How could she have thought him arrogant and cold? It was obvious now that he was in fact the complete opposite. He was desperately trying to deny his feelings so he could achieve his goals in the hope that would take away all the pain.

Trembling for what her realisation meant for her

attempts to shut down her own feelings for him, she stepped back so as not to disturb Marco. Accidentally bumping into one of the ICU nurses, she apologised profusely. But she'd given herself away. When she looked up again, Marco was standing, his eyes on her. He set the chair aside and fully opened the curtain around Fredo's bed.

'Dr Mancini,' he said, his dark stare turbulent.

'I came to check on him,' Elena said quietly, glancing at the still-sleeping man. 'Has there been any improvement?'

She'd hoped that work might help her to dismiss her feelings of hurt and disappointment, but standing this close to Marco brought everything back to the surface.

In answer to her enquiry, Marco shook his head. 'But these things take time, as you know. Can you please accompany me to my office. I wish to speak with you.'

They left ICU together, the awkwardness building with each step. For a thrilling moment as they entered his office, Elena wondered if he might drag her into his arms and kiss her, tell her that he'd changed his mind and wanted her still. But inside he left the door ajar, and her stomach sank.

Reaching for a flash drive on his desk, he passed it to Elena. 'I wanted you to have this.'

'What is this?' she asked, resentful of the desk behind which he had retreated. Was he worried she might throw herself at him again?

'It's a reference, signed by both myself and Dr Brienza. I've also emailed it to you. Your locum position here is coming to an end. I assume that you still plan to leave Capri and head back to Naples.'

She nodded numbly as unease slithered through her veins like ice, his gesture and reminder as harsh as a slap. But this was the jolt she needed. It was beautiful, but the luxurious guest house at the estate felt increasingly like a prison cell. Being so close to him but also so far away emotionally was slowly destroying her.

'I see you are eager to be rid of me.' She waved the flash drive, the contents as vile as hush money or worse because, despite what she'd said at the start, she hadn't been able to resist him physically. 'Thank you, I guess,' she said, tucking it into her pocket.

'That's not true. I simply urge you to one day continue your surgical training,' he continued in a controlled voice. 'You have the right skills for success.'

She nodded and glanced away. This was just another attempt at withdrawal for him. But it hurt all the same.

When she said nothing, he continued stiffly, 'Listen, I also wanted to apologise.' He stepped past her to fully close the door. 'For what happened that night in my study.'

Elena raised her chin and shot him a venomous look. She might also be trying to protect herself, her feelings, but she didn't regret what had happened between them in those snatched moments of honesty. She at least could own her desire for him.

'I should have controlled myself,' he said, his voice tight. 'I vowed it was over. I'm sorry.'

'*I'm* not,' she replied. 'I wanted you. I'm just sorry that I forgot to lock down my emotions. You are so much better at that than me.'

He swallowed, his hands twitching at his sides as if he might reach for her. But his jaw clenched instead, his expression hardened. 'That night you said you are nothing to me. That's not true. I care about you, Elena. For now, you are my wife. I do not want you to get hurt.'

'I don't want to hurt you either,' she said and his eyes widened for a split second as he grasped the implication of her words. That she saw his attempts to protect himself from her. But maybe Marco had walled up his heart so effectively he knew it was safe, knew she had no chance of even reaching it.

'I also want to apologise to you and your entire family,' he went on dispassionately. 'Before I met you, a part of me did hold the Medicina dell'Apparenza scandal responsible for my father's death. But I don't, of course, hold anyone personally responsible, least of all you. I want you to understand that.'

Elena sagged in defeat. 'I do understand, Marco.' Her eyes, locked to his, burned. 'I understand that needing to lay blame is a part of the grieving process. I didn't know it at the time, but when we met we were both grieving for our fathers.'

By agreeing to this sham marriage, she too had wanted to salvage something. But what she'd gained, or soon would, no longer felt like a victory. What she now wanted was murkier. More terrifying. Involved her trusting her own instincts once more when they had led her so wrong before.

She wanted to lay the past to rest for them both. She wanted Marco to find peace. And, riskiest of all, she wanted him to look at her the way he did when they were lost in each other physically.

But to want those things was to make herself vulnerable to him again, and she'd vowed when she'd left his study that she would protect herself better. She'd given her relationship with Rocco her all and it hadn't been enough. He'd betrayed her anyway, as if her love was worthless. How could she trust Marco with her heart when he couldn't trust her in return? Couldn't or wouldn't be fully vulnerable with her.

'Why were you sitting with Signore Degano?' she asked finally, unable to walk away when she could clearly see that Marco was hurting. Haunted by what he perceived as failures, perhaps.

'I am his surgeon,' he said in a clipped voice so she knew her instinct was correct. 'My clinical concern for my patient is entirely appropriate.' His stare intensified but he didn't move a muscle.

'Do you feel responsible for his current condition, for the pneumonia?' she asked, understanding him more than ever. Marco was a proud Italian man. Determined to always do the right thing and unfalteringly loyal to his family at any cost. 'Because ventilator-acquired pneumonia is a recognised complication of—'

She broke off when Marco held up his hand. 'I do not need you to tell me the statistics on post-operative complications, Dr Mancini.'

Elena squared her shoulders. 'Then do you need me to tell you that it isn't your fault? Just like the devastating loss of your father was not your fault. Nor was your messy divorce.'

Marco glanced down, his lips pressed together as if he now regretted sharing that with her in Rome. 'My failures are mine. I am Degano's consultant. I have ultimate responsibility for his care.' He looked up. 'When you have your own patients one day, you will understand fully the weight of that responsibility.'

Elena's heart sank. Somehow, despite his apologies and his display of tenderness at Fredo's bedside, he had reverted to the guarded robot of old.

'I understand that you are driven to be the best surgeon you can be. Driven to honour your father. But—'

'And you are not?' he interrupted.

'Of course I am. But at least I will talk about Papà. Express my feelings. Work through the grief I think you are allowing to hold you back. I know this, you and me, isn't a real relationship, that you can't even trust me, but maybe it is time we laid the Caruso-Mancini past to rest. After all, hasn't it cost us enough? I think both our fathers would want us to be happy, not stuck in the past. If you ever need to talk about your father, I am willing to listen. Because I understand what you are going through. I am there myself. Watching my father fade before my eyes with each passing week.'

'And I am deeply sorry that you face that,' he said quietly. 'I wouldn't wish it on anyone.' But rather than elaborate, Marco checked his watch. 'I need to get to my clinic. Please check with the ICU team later today and report back to me on Signore Degano's progress.'

Elena nodded and stood tall while inside some part of her withered at his dismissal. 'I will, Dr Caruso.'

She turned away, left his office, her heart aching for them both after everything they'd endured. But maybe his continued refusal to confide in her proved she was wrong. Maybe they were not so alike after all. Because where she wanted to work with him to resolve the past and their trust issue, to explore the feelings knowing him had wrought, Marco, by contrast, seemed intent on only pushing her away.

CHAPTER THIRTEEN

By the middle of the following week, Marco feared he might be in hell. His obsession with his wife had reached new heights, almost surpassing his obsession with the cancer centre. Her constant presence at work, the lovely smile she bestowed on patients and staff, glimpses of her around the estate in some filmy sundress or other taunted him and his resolve that their physical relationship was over. Or that he was even remotely in control of his feelings.

His home had become a place of agonising reminders. He saw her everywhere: the pool, the gym, the gardens, his study. His only reprieve was when she visited Naples at the weekends and then, perversely, he missed her, eagerly watching the clock until Sunday evening when, through the estate's security cameras, he saw Enzo dropping her home from the ferry. Her return meant two things. Not only was she still committed to this charade of an arrangement, despite his appalling behaviour and lack of willpower, she was, more importantly, still willing to leave her father's side. Marco dreaded the day when she did not return because that would mean that Gio Mancini's condition had deteriorated or, worse still, that he'd passed. That Elena faced the kind of grief Marco himself knew all too well. He wished, for her sake, he could take that away.

Arriving back at the estate after a long run, during which he'd tried to exhaust himself so he might fall into a dreamless sleep and not think about Elena, Marco passed the guest house. He kept his stare averted, praying she wasn't outside on the terrace. If he saw her, a fresh cycle of torment and denial would begin. But he was only a man. He'd already proved himself weak. At the last moment, he glanced over, spying her on the phone.

Her back was to him as she faced the view. She wore another light cotton sundress that was practically see-through against the setting sun. The glimpse of her gorgeous silhouette stirred his blood more effectively than the fifteen-kilometre run. But it was the tension in her shoulders, her arm gripped around her waist and her head bowed as if she was hearing bad news that brought his feet to a reluctant stop.

Instinctively, he went to her, dragging air into his burning lungs as fresh panic gripped him. It must be her father. It must be bad news. She would be devastated.

'*Ciao*,' she said before ending the call. Then her hand fell to her side, her fingers clenched around the phone as her shoulders slumped.

'What is it?' he asked, his muscles trembling as he fought to catch his breath over the panicked thundering of his pulse.

Elena turned to face him, sadness and wariness in her stare. 'My father hasn't been able to talk at all today. Mamma is so upset.'

Marco stepped closer. 'I am so sorry, *cara*.'

At his term of endearment, her head jerked up, defiance and doubt blazing in her eyes. She swallowed, clearly struggling to fight tears.

Without thinking, Marco folded his arms around her shoulders and held her close, her delicate warmth against him like a gasp of breath after being too long underwater. She smelled like summer and lemon blossom and he closed his eyes against the surge of desire for her as he tried to offer comfort.

'What can I do?' he pleaded, indulgently and discreetly inhaling the scent of her shampoo as he stroked one hand over her hair. It was dangerous, forbidden, selfish, but he couldn't seem to stop himself.

'Nothing,' she replied in defeat, her face on his chest. 'There is nothing anyone can do.'

Marco winced, frustrated because she was right. But seeing her suffer tore him to shreds. He stroked her back, aware that he was a sweaty mess. Not that she seemed to care as she accepted his embrace.

With her heart beating against his, the constant restlessness inside him quietened. The chatter in his head ceased, self-talk that urged him to push himself harder, achieve his goals faster, make things right for all his past mistakes, make his father and his family proud.

Elena's grip around his waist tightened just before she released him and extricated herself from his arms. She looked up at him, her stunning eyes brimming with pain and acceptance and strength. Her soft, normally smiling lips pressed together in a line.

Some invisible force gripped him. Before he even knew what he was doing, he dipped his head and gently brushed her lips with his.

'Don't,' she said, stepping further away. 'You said it was done. You said you didn't want to hurt me. You can't push me away, just to reel me back in. I'm not a toy. I won't be…humiliated and then rejected.'

'I'm sorry.' Marco winced, rubbed his hand over his face, devastated that he'd inadvertently made her feel how she must have felt with her ex. 'You're right. I just… I forgot myself. I can't bear to see you upset.' He gripped her face between his palms. 'But I am not using you, Elena. Why do you think I've forced myself to stay away when every inch of me craves you like an addict? I know I shouldn't, because I'm the one who insisted it was over, but I ache for you, constantly. I can't think straight… But I don't want to lead you on. I'm trying to protect you. I'm not in the right headspace for a relationship. I can't stop wanting you but nor can I give you what you deserve. Not until I've built something from the rubble of what we've both lost. Don't you see…?'

'We are both hurting,' she whispered, blinking against the shine in her eyes. 'Both wanting the other but denying ourselves. But I think it's out of fear, Marco. Fear to trust, to let another person in when we've been so wrong before. Fear that next time, it has to be right.'

Marco frowned at how clearly she saw him, his heart thudding that she still wanted him too.

'I'm scared for you, Marco,' she said, her stare searching his. 'Completing the clinic won't bring your father back, any more than me being the perfect doting daughter will save mine. These are things we must face alone if there is no way for us to face them together…'

Fighting himself, fighting her insights, Marco turned away from her and paced to the edge of the terrace to get some distance and think. Maybe she was right. Maybe they did finally need to address the past. He sighed. These views had always brought him comfort. But ever since Elena Mancini had walked into his life, their power had dulled. Now, the only moment of light-heartedness he experienced was when he caught sight of her smile, before she noticed him watching and frowned because he'd hurt her.

'My father loved it here,' he said, picking at his wound because Elena deserved so much more than he had given by constantly pushing her away. Even faced with her own father's dwindling health, she was also thinking of Marco. 'But he also loved his work. When he spent parts of the week in Naples or Rome, we missed him, of course, but we were also proud of his reputation as a plastic surgeon. The successful clinics all over Italy, including for a while, Medicina dell'Apparenza.'

When he turned around, Elena silently observed him wearing another hesitant frown, her arms crossed. Despite his best attempts not to, he'd hurt her anyway by his need for her physically.

'When that patient sued,' he choked out, guilt making it easier to open up, 'my father wanted to settle. Even though he knew Gio was also a good doctor and had done everything right. Now that I know you, his daughter, I have no doubt that Gio Mancini had done his best as a surgeon.'

And who was Marco to judge another doctor? Sometimes intervention versus inaction necessitated walking a delicate tightrope, the judgement calls brutal.

'But Papà wanted to fight the litigation,' she said with a sigh of defeat that tore him open. 'I get my stubborn streak from him.'

'Dario explained to Gio the potential risks of a public court case, the risks to the clinic if things didn't go Gio's way,' Marco continued. 'Caruso Enterprises and their share of Medicina dell'Apparenza were well protected. My father was lucky enough to have both business experience and generational wealth on which to fall back.'

'And mine had no such luxury.' She hung her head, her sadness crushing him. Then she looked up with that fire he admired and adored. 'My father was reckless, not half the businessman of yours. But he believed in standing on principle. He'd exhaustively explained the risks of that new surgical technique to the patient, so in his mind, the civil case was unfair. But what destroyed him the most was when Dario made that public statement, distancing himself from the decisions Gio had made. He considered Dario a friend and that betrayal cut deep.'

When she looked away, he went to her, tilting up her chin so their eyes met. 'For what it's worth, I know Dario regretted that decision to the day he died. He'd felt compelled to give a public statement to try and mitigate the damage. Sometimes aggrieved patients just want an apology. He was a traditionalist. He stuck to tried and tested methods. He was an honest man and couldn't lie, but he gave his surgical opinion of the technique Gio had used, knowing that he was also betraying a friend and valued colleague. It tore him up.'

'I think on some level Papà understood that,' she said, nodding as she blinked. 'But the same pride that stopped him from settling the case quietly out of court also led him to break off any contact with Dario after he'd issued his statement. I think he found it easier to blame your father for disloyalty than to blame himself for the horrible public position into which he'd forced his family and yours.'

'Dario too felt his responsibilities. To his family, his patients, to me his son, a younger surgeon who emulated his success. It was a horrible time for us all.'

'You looked up to him?' she said softly, her lips trembling. He wanted to still them with a kiss, but dared not.

He nodded. 'Of course. He'd always been there for me. He even bailed me out over my ex-wife's divorce demands.'

'He did?' She frowned and Marco sighed, his throat tight at the notion of raking over one of his deepest regrets.

'I told you how she went after everything in the divorce settlement. Well, she also employed Europe's toughest legal team. I made her a generous settlement offer, which she rejected. She tried to go after a share of everything. Not just half of the homes we'd bought together. She dragged my entire family into the fight. The Caruso estate belonged to my grandfather but she knew it would one day be mine. And we'd temporarily lived there when we were first married. Logically, I knew she would eventually be unsuccessful, but Dario encouraged me to cut my losses rather than drag the divorce out over years.'

He swallowed hard, recalling the shame and frustration he'd battled at the time. 'He had already been diagnosed with cancer at this stage. None of us needed the additional stress of another public fight and lengthy legal battle. With his financial assistance, I made Bianca a more generous counter-offer. I gave her both of our homes, one in Rome and one in Tuscany, and most of my shares in Caruso Enterprises as a final settlement and moved back here to live with my grandfather.'

'I'm sorry,' she whispered. 'That must have been very distracting. I can't believe she would treat you so…ruthlessly.'

He shook his head. 'I don't regret it. My father was right. What I cannot forgive is how she came for me and my family at the most unimaginably painful time. Nor can I forgive myself. My father faced surgery and chemotherapy. He should have been focused on fighting his disease, not bailing me out for my mistake of a marriage. I added to his stress at a time when I should have been caring for him.' He turned away from her, shame for all his bad choices almost crushing.

'It wasn't your fault,' she said, stepping up behind him and pulling him to face her once more.

'I will never know,' he choked out. 'But I know I let my loved ones down. That's why I need to do something that puts this family back together again before I can even think about myself.'

She stepped forward and placed her hand on his chest over his heart. 'I understand you, Marco. I too made a mistake and loved the wrong person. And we have all lost something through the Medicina dell'Apparenza affair.'

Marco nodded. 'My father might have emerged financially unscathed, but his reputation also took a hit and within months he'd been diagnosed with cancer.'

'Papà doesn't know,' she whispered, her eyes tortured. 'I'm scared to tell him about your father's passing. They were both proud men, and I can't bear the thought of upsetting Papà in his final weeks.'

'Then keep it to yourself, *cara*,' he urged. 'It's like you said—it wasn't our fight.'

She nodded, her stare searching his. 'You didn't let your family down, Marco. Were your father here right now, he would be so proud of you. Of the man you are and of the professional reputation you have built up over years of hard work and dedication. He would be proud of your plans to finish the Caruso Cancer Centre. But he would also want you to be happy. We both need to put the mistakes of the past behind us and be happy, don't you think?'

Elena watched doubt and fear darken Marco's troubled stare. 'You said I don't talk about him,' he said, 'but that's because it hurts. My failure of a marriage, my divorce, hurt my father when he was sick. I let him down at the worst possible time. I can't fail again.'

Elena shook her head against each of his statements. 'You won't fail. You are a highly respected surgeon, just like your father was. You will succeed in creating a legacy for him and yourself and your family. Just remember that you deserve things too.

A second chance. Love. A family of your own, if you want that. Don't put yourself last for ever.'

Because she couldn't stand the heartbreakingly vulnerable look on his face, because he'd finally opened himself up and finally let her in, she stepped close and held his face. 'I'm sorry for everything you've been through.'

His arms came around her. 'I'm sorry for all that you have been through too. That's why I'm trying to resist this. I can't give you anything right now. And it's not about you. It's about *me*. I pushed you away because I'm damaged. Don't you see? I've messed up before. I tried to be a good husband, but my best wasn't enough. And until I have laid my father properly to rest, made amends for my failures, I cannot give you or anyone else what you might need.'

'I know,' Elena said, allowing him to hold her and comfort her because he'd finally given her what she'd yearned for and let her in.

Part of her wished they'd met at a different time, when they had each healed from the betrayals of the past. But knowing him, working for him, discovering Dario's fate had helped her put things into perspective. Love was all that mattered. Right now, she needed to focus on her family. But one day, she would be ready to risk her heart again for love. And next time, she'd get it right.

'I'm leaving at the end of next week for Naples,' she said, looking up at him. 'When I go, I'll leave behind everything that happened between us and focus on my family for however long Papà has left.'

'And I will miss you.' He frowned, a flash of uncertainty in his eyes. Because whatever this had been, their time was running out. 'Not just at work.'

'I'll miss you too, Marco.' She surged onto her tiptoes and pressed her lips to his. 'But I won't let you hurt me,' she said, her pulse buzzing as she cupped his face. 'Because you are right. I do deserve more. I deserve everything. When I'm ready, I want a man who loves and adores me and can give me all of himself in return for all of me.'

'Elena…' he groaned, his hands on her hips. He clenched his jaw and swallowed as if pained. 'I…'

She pressed her fingers to his lips. 'Don't. I don't need promises you can't keep. I know what this is between us. I have always known. We made an arrangement, remember.'

She understood his trust issues, because she had them too. She understood family loyalty and preserving a legacy for those you loved. She understood how hard it was to repair damaged trust.

'I just want to pretend for a while longer, until I leave.' She slid her lips along his stubbled jaw to his earlobe and down his neck.

She was willing to put herself at risk in the fire and deal with consequences when he was out of sight. Until then, she wouldn't think about reality. She would take solace from the fact that in addressing their fathers' controversy they'd resolved some of the pain of the past. And by finally letting her in, she hoped to help Marco through his grief before it was over.

With an agonised groan of surrender, Marco fisted the fabric of her dress at her hips. He crushed her to him and kissed her, pushing his tongue against hers so she sagged against his hard chest.

'You are certain?' he said when he pulled back, his stare dark with arousal and doubt.

'Yes.' She nodded and in the next second, he filled his hands with the cheeks of her backside and hoisted her from the floor.

'Hold on.'

Elena clung to him as he carried her across the terrace and into the cool living room. In another four or five determined strides he lowered her to the bed she'd been using and dropped to his knees, peeling her underwear off and then her dress.

She shivered as she watched him strip. Not because she was cold. A warm scented breeze entered via the open French windows. But the intent look on his face, the speed at which he removed his clothing, told her he was, like her, dangerously on edge. By denying this, they'd each suffered. But they were adults. As long as they were honest, they could indulge this physical need while also protecting themselves.

He tossed aside his running shorts and underwear and joined her on the bed, prowling over her to lay frantic kisses and roaming hands all over her body. 'I tried so hard to stop wanting you.'

'Marco…' she moaned as he captured her nipple with his mouth. 'I need you.'

He trailed his tongue down her abdomen and between her legs, dragging another desperate cry from her throat. Then he gave her what she wanted, joining them with a slow thrust that filled her and sent her body weak with pleasure.

'I tried so hard,' he said, gently pushing her hair back from her flushed face. 'I fought it. Over and over. But I'm weak. You make me weak.'

She shook her head, holding his cheeks between her palms. 'I tried too. I even tried to hate you for your impressive resolve, but failed.'

'My resolve led me here, *cara*. Here with you. Needing you more than I need my next breath.'

'Marco,' she whispered, sliding her mouth back to his, kissing him deeply to match his possession of her body as he dragged moan after moan from her throat and spasm after delicious spasm from her core.

She came, surrounded by him, consumed, burning up. He held her so tight through every second of pleasure, harshly grunting her name as he climaxed too and the furious pressure of the past couple of weeks snapped at last.

CHAPTER FOURTEEN

MARCO SHIFTED UNDERNEATH a naked Elena, the cooling breeze from the open window raising goosebumps on her arms.

'I'm sweaty,' he said, still raw from his earlier confession on the terrace. From the fight and surrender of wanting her. From the intensity of them together and how it somehow silenced all of his doubts for a while. Doubts that he might be falling apart. Doubts that by selfishly craving his wife he would hurt her when this ended. Doubts that maybe she was right and his obsession with the cancer centre would not fulfil him the way he hoped.

'Who cares?' she said, raising her dishevelled head to press a kiss to his chest.

His body reacted to her touch. An impressive feat for a man in his forties who'd just run fifteen kilometres and a sexual duathlon. But after denying himself Elena for so long, one time just hadn't been enough.

'You are right, you know,' he said, his gut griping with fear at how uncontrollable this thing between them was. 'You do deserve what you said earlier—a man who loves and adores you.'

The idea of that future man, a better man than

him, knifed him, but he was desperate to think of something, anything, other than how *he* would ever stop wanting this woman. Even her promise that she would not allow herself to get hurt was not enough to allow him to breathe easy.

He'd been so focused on honouring his father for so long, he feared if he tried to do it all, have it all, tried to give Elena more than the scraps he'd given her so far, he'd mess up again. Make another mistake. Hurt his family once more. Lose something else that was irreplaceable, the way he'd lost his father.

Elena sighed and burrowed closer. 'I do, but I'm also scared to get it wrong again. Rocco was fun and charming, polite and respectful to my family. I fell hard for him.'

Her honest statement felt like a kick in the ribs, even though Marco had been expecting it. Elena would love with her whole heart and deserved a man who could do the same in return.

'We talked about marriage and the size of family we might have, and I was convinced that he'd been about to propose when my father and Medicina dell'Apparenza were served the lawsuit.'

It was hard to listen to her dreams for two reasons. One, the jealousy of her loving this man who had let her down, but harder still was the knowledge of Elena's pain and betrayal, which he felt echo deep within him as if it were his own. Just like it had physically pained him to see her sadness over Gio.

'Obviously, as the case garnered more and more publicity,' she continued, 'the headlines became more damaging, I could see that Rocco felt torn. It was a conflict for him to write anything about my father, but I naïvely thought he was just being pressured to pursue the story. By the time the case came to court, Rocco had begun to distance himself from me emotionally.

'He claimed to be busy with work, but I suspected he was struggling with his association with us as a family. To me. I felt ashamed by all the bad press so I assumed he was simply embarrassed and keeping his head down. But there must have been good money to be made from an inside scoop, and one day he just announced that he'd written it ahead of its publication the next day.'

Marco tightened his arms around her protectively. 'I'm sorry, *cara*.'

She shivered and shook her head. 'I begged him not to publish but he chose his career over me. I thought he loved me. I needed him. It felt as if my family was falling apart, but instead of standing by me, he callously contributed to the stress we were under with his story. He walked away from our two-year relationship as easily as tossing rubbish into the bin.'

'That's horrible. Unforgivable.' And he'd thought Bianca ruthless…

'Of course,' she continued, 'he, along with every other journalist in Naples, wrote about the conclusion of the case and the judgement and subsequent bankruptcy of Mancini Holdings. So his betrayal became absolute, and I learned hard lessons about who I could trust.'

'No one deserves to be publicly eviscerated or treated so callously,' Marco said, guilt rumbling in his chest, because he'd allowed their fathers' past to cloud things and had also unfairly judged her when they'd first met. But how wrong he'd been. Elena was extraordinary. She'd taught him so much about the past, about grief and forgiveness.

'No.' She sighed. 'I just wish I'd seen through him sooner. Realised my mistake. Seen how shallow he was and how easily his loyalty, his feelings, if he ever had any for me, could be shaken. But I've learned my lesson. Next time I'm ready to risk my heart again, it will be for the right person. Next time I marry—' she looked up with a heartbreaking smile '—for real, I mean, it will be with a man who knows exactly who I am but adores me anyway.'

Marco stilled, his heart thudding and throat tight at the picture she painted. 'You have nothing to regret, *cara*. You did nothing wrong and deserve so much better than a man so two-faced and heartless. It's not a mistake to love with your whole heart. It's not your fault, or mine, that our exes said one thing then changed and became different people when times were tough.' He cupped her face. 'You are so strong. I know you won't destroy who you are just to protect yourself from being hurt again.'

It was only that strength, along with her reassurances that he couldn't be the man for her, that had finally allowed him to be with her again.

She shook her head and whispered, 'You shouldn't either.'

Marco held his breath, stunned again by this incredible woman's ability to see him so clearly.

'Anyway…' she said, ducking her eyes when Marco stayed silent, 'my upset over a broken heart soon became eclipsed by Papà's diagnosis. I love my father. I hate his disease. But it gave me no time to wallow in my own regrets over an unworthy man.'

Marco brushed his lips over hers, needing her kiss every bit as much as he wished he could take away all of her pain.

'He reached out to me a few months ago,' she said as an afterthought when she pulled back. 'Rocco.'

Marco slowly exhaled and tried to stop his body from stiffening. 'What did he want?'

'To apologise. He'd heard about Papà's diagnosis and obviously felt guilty. Or maybe he just wanted another story.'

'Did you respond?' he asked, something dark twisting inside him.

'No. I have nothing to say to him.'

'Have you…told anyone about our arrangement? About the marriage?' What if her journalist ex sniffed around and discovered what they'd done? One slip-up could jeopardise everything: the inheritance, the clinic, Gio Mancini's peace of mind in his final weeks.

'No.' She frowned. 'I promised I wouldn't. I haven't even told Dino yet.'

'Why not?' Marco frowned, confused by her silence and what it meant. She would need to tell Dino when he handed over the Dignità shares.

'He won't be able to keep a secret,' she said, 'and Mamma can only think about my father at the moment. She wouldn't understand what I've done.' She ducked her gaze once more. 'She'd think it was a romantic decision. She'd worry about me getting hurt again.'

'I don't want that… I—'

'I'm a grown woman, Marco. I know what I'm doing. I stand by my decisions and face the consequences. I told you, I'm not looking for a promise you can't keep. Believe me, I've been there before and I won't go there again.'

Marco's chest ached as he cupped her face, his restlessness returning, despite the fact she was perfect and in his arms and saying all the right things. 'You are an incredible woman. You deserve everything you want.'

She nodded, a glimmer of sadness in her eyes. 'So do you.'

He held her close, his gut churning. He'd been so focused on making amends since Dario's death, he hadn't once stopped to think about what he wanted, beyond making the Caruso Cancer Centre a reality. But of course he had personal dreams. He did want love again one day. He even wanted a family. He would not lead Elena on, but if their timing had been different, if he had already worked through his grief and regrets…

Might they have had a chance at a real relationship?

The next week passed in a busy and passionate blur Elena spent each day trying not to overanalyse. She and Marco worked together by day and sought out each other at night. Eating dinner together on the terrace, learning new things about each other, sleeping together. As if by mutual agreement, they avoided further discussions of the past and any mention of the future. Finally laying the Caruso-Mancini history to rest seemed to give them permission to simply live in the moment, as if they could each hear every second of the ticking clock. And since the night they'd shared Elena's bed, they hadn't spent one apart.

Back in Theatre together, they each sutured a mastectomy wound on a patient with bilateral breast cancer, slowly and methodically closing the chest wounds as aesthetically as possible.

They were washing their hands at the sinks outside Theatre Three when Elena's phone rang.

'Dr Mancini,' she said, glancing to Marco when the ICU doctor spoke, as if she could communicate by look alone.

After a brief conversation, she hung up and relayed the pertinent information to Marco. 'Signore Degano's oxygen saturations are dipping and his latest blood tests show renal dysfunction. The ICU consultant wants to intubate him for ventilation.'

Marco frowned, most likely thinking the same as Elena. Their patient didn't seem to be responding to any of their treatment, and ventilation most definitely felt like another backwards step.

'Let's go,' Marco said, hurrying from Theatres and heading for the stairs with Elena at his side.

On ICU they met with the specialist. 'His blood pressure has been on the low side,' Dr Lombardi told them. 'His fever spiked again last night. We have repeated the blood cultures. Obviously, we are concerned about septicaemia. And I think he has a small pleural effusion.'

'Have you repeated a chest X-ray?' Marco asked his colleague.

'Yes. The results should be through now. Let's take a look.' Dr Lombardi checked the computer and brought up the latest digital image.

'It *is* a pleural effusion,' Elena said, observing the chest X-ray. Half of the lung on the affected side was obscured by 'white-out', an indication of fluid in the chest cavity. 'Could be an empyema.' Sometimes in cases of pneumonia, pus collected in the pleural space.

Marco nodded, agreeing with Elena's observation. 'Want to pop a chest drain in and see what we're dealing with?'

'Of course,' she said, awash with the sensation of professional camaraderie. She finally felt like a vital and respected member of Marco's team.

While an ICU nurse collected the equipment they would need, they each examined Fredo, who appeared increasingly frail every time Elena visited.

'We need to place a drain in your chest, Signore Degano,' Marco explained. 'There is a build-up of fluid.'

With the patient positioned on the bed, Elena pulled on sterile gloves and swabbed the skin of his lateral chest wall under the patient's armpit. Finding the space between the fifth and sixth ribs, Elena injected local anaesthetic and then, with Marco watching on, slowly and carefully inserted the chest tube.

The moment the drain entered the pleural space, yellow fluid filled the tube.

'The effusion is purulent,' she told Marco, who asked the nurse to collect a sample for the microbiology lab.

'Well done, Signore Degano,' Elena said after stitching, and taped the chest tube in place. She connected the end to the collection bottle and then helped the nurses get the patient comfortable once more.

'I am sure that will improve things,' Marco said, resting his hand on Fredo's shoulder. 'Dr Mancini will organise some further tests and I'll return to see you later this evening.'

After they stepped away from the bedside, he told Elena, 'I need to get back to Theatre. Can you repeat the chest X-ray and blood gas analysis? That drain will help the situation, I'm sure, but if he requires ventilation, that's the call we'll have to make.' He frowned, his gaze returning to the patient.

'I'll call Signora Degano and explain this latest development, if you like,' she said, wishing they could find a moment to be alone so she could touch him and let him know that, despite this latest setback for their patient, they were in this together. That he didn't have to shoulder all the responsibility alone. That she was there for him as well as their patients.

'Thank you,' he said, his stare holding hers for a handful of seconds so she witnessed things she wanted to be true. That he cared for her was obvious. He didn't want her to get hurt. And since the night they'd shared her bed at the guest house, she'd clung to counting down the days in order to protect herself. But despite guarding her own feelings, she also knew she wanted so much more of Marco than he was willing to give. If only he could risk another real relationship, if only she could be confident they wanted the same things, she could so easily fall for him.

'Leave it to me,' she said and watched him hurry back to Theatre. For now, all she could do to help

Marco and this patient who had come to mean so much to her was to do her job to the best of her abilities and hope that it would be enough.

Because when she walked away at the weekend, it had to be for ever.

CHAPTER FIFTEEN

AFTER ANOTHER NIGHT in Marco's arms, another night where she shut down any feelings so she could have the only part of him that was on offer, Elena arrived at work the next day shocked to find a huddle of journalists camped on the pavement opposite the SMC entrance. As she hurried inside, her head down, cameras popped and her name was called. She was used to ignoring them because of her past, but were they there for her? Surely there was no mileage left in her father's story. Unless they'd finally heard about her and Marco's high-profile patient…

Her stomach churned, the incident triggering memories of another time, when she hadn't been able to leave the house without some journalist or photographer pushing her for a comment on the court ruling or her father's summons to pay compensation to the patient.

Elena hurried to ICU to review Fredo Degano before she spent the rest of the day in Dr Brienza's follow-up clinic.

As she walked onto ICU, a couple of the nurses looked up from a computer screen, flashing her a guilty smile.

'What's going on?' she asked them quietly. 'Why are there press outside?'

'They want a statement regarding Signore Degano,' his nurse said. 'Somehow they discovered he's a patient here.'

Elena came around the desk and glanced at the computer, which showed a headline in *Novità Oggi*, one of the national newspapers. *Former Politician Clinging to Life in ICU* the article claimed, and the byline made Elena's blood run cold. *Rocco Conti.* Her ex.

Just then, Marco strode onto the ward, his expression controlled and professional. Certainly no hint of the man who'd made love to her at the crack of dawn as the sun rose. The man who'd lazily kissed her goodbye and promised that for their final night together on Capri he wanted them to share one last dinner on the terrace.

'Shall we review Signore Degano together?' he said to Elena and Fredo's nurse before he strode off.

Elena stood at the patient's bedside, making notes, informing Marco of the latest test results and microbiology reports, waiting for a moment when they were alone so they could discuss the latest development: the press outside.

'I believe we have turned the corner on this infection,' Marco told the patient, a hint of his gorgeous smile tugging at his mouth so Elena's heart clenched at how much warmer his bedside manner now was. 'You keep on improving and we'll soon have you off ICU and can work towards getting you home. Signora Degano misses you, as do all those grandchildren of yours.'

With the review over, Marco and Elena left ICU together.

'Can I speak to you in my office?' he asked, his voice clipped with efficiency as if he was distracted. 'It will only take a moment.' But of course they were all distracted by the story in the papers.

Elena closed the door behind them and went to him. 'I assume you've seen the press outside? The article? Poor Signora Degano. This is typical of Rocco. He just doesn't care about the human angle or the people behind the headlines.'

His jaw clenched. 'So I am right in thinking that this Rocco Conti, the journalist who somehow knows everything about our patient, is your ex?'

'Yes,' she said, prickles of dread dancing over her skin. Why was he looking at her that way, without a single emotion displayed on his face? 'But I told you what he's like. How…ruthless he can be for a story. It's a horrible coincidence, but—'

'I'm not sure I believe in coincidences,' he interrupted, his voice so cold it made Elena shiver. 'There is no way anyone could have discovered Signore Degano was here by accident. SMC prides itself on privacy and discretion. And Degano and I discussed him delaying any sort of public statement he might make about his cancer journey until after he had completed his treatment, so the leak could not have come from one of his team.'

'Marco…' she said, hating the pleading note in her voice. 'What are you saying?' What was he accusing her of? 'You think I'm the leak, don't you?' she gasped out when he didn't reply, the pain of Marco's lack of belief in her twisting her stomach.

'Are you?' His expression was stony and remote.

'No! Of course not. I can't believe that you even need to ask.' Elena felt winded. As if she'd been punched. She shouldn't have to defend herself. She'd told him about Rocco's betrayal. About her devastation and the impact of being the subject of those headlines on her family. 'I care about all my patients and respect Signore Degano too much to ever contemplate such a horrible betrayal. How could you think that?'

But any other words he might now speak no longer mattered. The damage was done. While she'd been loving him with her body and opening up her battered, wary heart, trying to heal the past and help him through his grief, Marco hadn't changed at all. He was still the same man she'd called a robot. Still untrusting and suspicious.

'You did say he'd reached out to you recently,' he continued. 'What was I supposed to think?'

'So what? You think I betrayed you and my professionalism? Why would I do that?'

He looked down and it struck her with the force of another blow.

'You think I did it to get back at you, Dario Caruso's son, for what your father did to mine… That's what you believed, isn't it?'

When he simply stared, neither denying or confirming, she realised he would never trust her. Ever.

She blinked rapidly, her eyes stinging and her throat burning with a horrible sense of betrayal that she'd experienced before when she'd loved the wrong man. And despite what she'd promised, how she'd tried to protect herself, she feared she was already falling for Marco.

'I haven't spoken to my ex or seen him in two years,' she said, feeling sick. 'You asked what you were supposed to think and it's this, Marco. You're supposed to believe in me. I've never once given you any reason not to. I… I foolishly thought you trusted me.'

Marco swallowed, his stare hard. 'I did. I do. But we both know we can never truly know what is in another person's heart. You said it yourself.'

Elena stepped closer, her hands itching to shake this withdrawn version of Marco until the real man emerged. The man she'd been falling for, day by day.

'Well, I trusted *you*,' she said, her voice strangled as she tried to battle the sickening injustice and humiliation of his unfounded accusations. 'I confided in you about my past because I thought you cared about me.'

As pain burned under her ribs, she saw it all so

clearly. Would she feel this crushed by his baseless accusation unless her feelings were involved?

Rather than hear the sincerity of her declaration, Marco scowled. 'I do—' He broke off, swallowing hard so when his voice next emerged it was flat with resolve. 'But…this is a scandal no one needs. As soon as the press outside sniff around, they will discover that you and I have been working together to care for Signore Degano. A Caruso and a Mancini. I will need to clean up this mess…'

Elena absorbed the second blow like a prize-fighter in the ring. 'So you're ashamed to be associated with me now. Is that it? Because of the past. Because I'm Gio Mancini's daughter?' Her blood boiled. Not only was he unjustly accusing her of something she didn't do, he was also hoping to distance himself, just as his father had done to Gio.

'I'm not ashamed, but when word gets out that we have been working together, the Medicina dell'Apparenza case will be regurgitated. This will not look good for SMC. Nor will it be good for your father.'

Elena hung her head, her stomach twisted. Marco was right; the last thing her family needed was to find themselves back in the papers. 'Of course, you're probably also worried it might damage your plans for the Caruso Cancer Centre,' she said flatly. It was a cruel blow, but her temper had been unleashed. 'Maybe you can release a statement blaming me for Signore Degano's post-op complications.'

'Do not be absurd,' he said calmly. 'I told you I am responsible for my patients.'

'Well, don't worry,' she said, her legs weak. 'I am leaving tomorrow as planned. So any embarrassing association will be short-lived.'

Marco stared, his lips pressed together. For a thrilling moment as his stare searched hers, she thought he might drag her into his arms as he'd done at dawn. Declare the feelings she was now certain she had for him, but he did not have for her.

He sighed and her stomach fell. 'Let's not say anything more we might regret,' Marco suggested reasonably. 'Why don't we discuss this later? At home.'

His pager sounded and he glanced at it with frustration. 'I need to go. I'm late for my first surgery, having spent the morning with hospital management discussing a press release strategy.' He stepped closer, hesitation in his expression.

For a euphoric moment she thought he might promise that they would figure this mess out together. Not that it would be enough. Now that she'd seen how easily shaken his trust was, she wanted more. She wanted to know if he could ever do more than simply care about her. She wanted to know his feelings for her. But maybe he had already shown her. In his wary looks. His suspicion and disappointment. The things he'd left unsaid.

He moved to the door and pulled it open. Before

he could leave, Elena uttered one last desperate plea. 'It wasn't me.'

He glanced back, the preoccupied look on his face telling her his thoughts were already elsewhere. 'At this stage, it does not matter who the leak was. I am Degano's lead clinician. The buck stops with me.'

Elena watched him leave, her shoulders slumped in defeat as something fragile inside her cracked. Had she, yet again, made another mistake in trusting the wrong man? She'd tried to stop herself, but she'd developed feelings for him. A man so practised in locking down his own emotions. A man who, despite what they'd shared these past weeks, despite the legal document making them husband and wife, could never fully trust her.

Later that night, in the privacy of the guest house on the estate, Elena checked the time and then paced back to the bathroom. Some time during her hectic day, a day where she'd had to say goodbye to all her patients, including Signore Degano, she'd realised that she hadn't had a period in the whole time she'd been on Capri. There had been that one weekend when she'd visited Naples but left her pills at the estate so she'd missed taking a couple. So on the way home from work, with fear and sadness a dull ache inside, she'd purchased several pregnancy tests.

In the bathroom of the guest house, she picked

up the test stick with a trembling hand and read the result: pregnant.

She covered her mouth and gasped, her eyes swimming with tears of both wonder and heartache. She was going to have Marco's baby. A wave of immediate love rose in her, only to be squashed by the doubts she'd battled since their sickening argument that morning.

As she stared at the result, a second realisation followed, one that stole her breath and left her trembling. She was in love with her husband. Deeply and absolutely.

Adrenaline surged through her. How could she have been so…careless? He'd told her over and over that there was no place for feelings in their marriage, but she'd fallen in love with him anyway. With a man who couldn't love her back. Couldn't even trust her. A man consumed by his father's legacy, haunted by his failures and so desperate to protect himself from being hurt that, at the first sign of trouble, he'd shut down his feelings and shut Elena out.

Whereas she'd opened up to him, told him about her past heartache and betrayal, about her fears and grief for her father. She'd even tried to help him deal with *his* grief while experiencing her own.

And in return he'd judged her unfairly, accused her of something dreadful and unprofessional and pushed her away again, hurting her when he'd said he wouldn't.

Glancing in the mirror, Elena studied her reflection, forcing herself to see the truth. Maybe Marco wasn't simply suppressing his feelings. Maybe he wasn't trying to protect her from being hurt. Maybe she'd deluded herself again. Maybe Marco had no feelings for her, just like Rocco.

Dropping her hand to her stomach, she raised her chin. Now, more than ever, she needed to be strong. This was no longer just about her and Marco, their feelings or their pasts. This was about their baby, the future. She would get over their divorce, over her broken heart. After all, she'd survived that before. All that mattered now was that she protected their child. And for the next nine months until it was born, that meant taking care of herself.

CHAPTER SIXTEEN

AFTER A LONG day operating and more questions from the hospital press office, Marco returned to the estate, his mind scrambled. Hospital management had been furious about the leak to the press. SMC prided itself on discretion and privacy for its patients and their failure to protect Marco's high-profile patient had trickled down to everyone involved in Degano's care. Marco believed Elena was innocent. But he blamed himself. If the man's post-operative recovery had gone more smoothly, Signore Degano might have been at home by now, recovering with his loved ones.

Pulling his car into the garage, and having seen the lights on as he'd passed, he headed for Elena's guest house. Unease rumbled in his gut. He'd behaved badly that morning. Unfairly accused her and hurt her feelings. It was no excuse, but he'd just had too many balls in the air and if he lost concentration, he feared he might drop them all.

Tapping at the door, he waited, needing to hold her and say goodbye for now, but not before he'd apologised.

Elena opened the door, her beautiful eyes wary as she took him in.

'Can I come in?' he asked. 'We should talk. I wanted to apologise.'

She nodded and stepped back and Marco followed her inside, his stomach twisting further when he saw her packed bags in the hall.

'I need to talk to you, too,' she said, wrapping her arms across her chest.

'First, let me say this,' he said, tiredly scrubbing a hand over his face. 'I'm sorry for accusing you. I know you would never betray a patient's privacy that way. I just… The hospital's press office summoned me first thing this morning. They had already researched Rocco Conti and, as you might expect, your name came up in stories from the past.'

She nodded, moving into the living area. 'I'm not surprised. But I don't care, Marco. I had to stop caring what other people thought of me, wrote about me and my family, a long time ago.'

Marco stepped closer, his body rigid and his hands twitching to touch her. 'I lashed out, Elena. I was feeling overwhelmed, but that's no excuse. I should not have even asked if the leak had come from you.' He placed his hands on her shoulders and squeezed. 'I do trust you. I'm sorry.'

'Marco,' she said, blinking up at him, 'I don't care about SMC or the press or my ex. I'm pregnant.'

'What?' Marco froze, his head spinning. 'I thought you were on the pill…'

'I am.' She lowered her gaze and stepped back so his arms fell to his sides. 'But what with all the travelling back and forth to Naples, I forgot to take a couple.' She looked up and raised her chin, that flash of challenge in her stare.

Marco's heart beat so fast, he struggled to draw breath. 'Are you…certain?'

'I've done three tests,' she said, the look she shot him dull with disappointment. Obviously, he wasn't handling this very well. 'I'm happy to do a fourth now if you want real-time proof.'

'I don't need proof.' He shook his head, his legs unsteady. He was going to be a father…

'Are you sure?' she pressed. 'I don't expect you to just believe me.'

Marco winced, taking another step towards her, one from which she recoiled. 'That's not fair. I do believe you, on both counts. Are you okay?' he asked, keeping his eyes on hers when his instinct was to drop them to her flat stomach where their baby grew.

'Physically, yes,' she said. 'Obviously, we need to figure out what we're going to do.'

'What do you want to do?' he asked, his throat tight because of course they'd never actually discussed having a child together. Maybe Elena didn't want a baby. 'This affects you the most. It's your body, your career. You have to give birth.'

'I want to have the baby,' she said, her chin rising. 'I'll figure everything else out.'

'*We'll* figure everything else out.' Unable to stay away from her a second longer, Marco crossed the room and drew her into his arms, his whirling mind still playing catch-up. Sighing with relief as he held her, 'I'm sorry,' he whispered, pressing his lips to her forehead. 'I should have taken better care of you.'

'Don't do that,' she said, pushing him away. 'This wasn't a mistake for me. I'm not saying that I planned the pregnancy, but nor do I have one second's regret.'

'Of course not,' he said, wincing because he seemed to be saying all the wrong things today. 'I'm not saying it's a mistake. I'm saying we're in this together. We'll figure it all out together.'

She shook her head and moved further away. Dread drained through him like ice.

'I'm still going back to Naples,' she said, not meeting his gaze.

'Of course…' he said. 'Let's have dinner and talk it all through before the morning. But you can come back to Capri. Maybe take some time off and rest here. Live in the guest house for as long as you like while we figure things out.'

She looked up, her disappointed expression leaving him even more confused.

'I can't do that, Marco,' she whispered. 'And I'm leaving tonight.'

'Why?' He frowned, desperation bubbling in his chest. 'If you leave pregnant,' he rushed on, 'it will definitely look suspicious. We've only been married a matter of weeks. The estate isn't officially mine yet. No one is going to believe that we're separated after such a short time when we have a child on the way.' He'd messed up this morning, let her down by doubting her. But he couldn't lose her, lose his baby… Not when he was juggling all these balls. When he was so close to making everything right. For his father, the estate, the future.

'I'm sorry.' Her eyes hardened and he saw that she'd come to this decision before he'd even knocked on the door. 'But I can't stay. I don't care what people think is suspicious.'

'But you promised,' he said, losing his grip on everything, his mind still whirling about the baby and Elena leaving that night. 'We had a deal,' he pleaded. 'An arrangement.' He couldn't let her leave like this. What if everything soured between them once she was in Naples and he lost her and his child for good?

She shook her head, cutting him off. 'Earlier, you said we never truly know what is in people's hearts. So I'll tell you exactly what's in mine.' Her voice was clear, her eyes shining with strength and fearless vulnerability. 'I love you, Marco.'

Marco froze, his heart surging into his throat even as his mind shut down. Overloaded. 'But… You said… You promised you understood…' His head was scrambled, the events of the day, the revelations tying him in knots he might never be able to untangle.

'I know. But I'm human,' she said, 'and I'm

deeply in love with you. I realised it today when I felt so destroyed by your lack of faith in me and again when I discovered that I'm having your baby.'

'Hold on… I'm catching up here…' An invisible band tightened around his chest, making it hard to breathe. 'I've just found out that we're having a baby on top of a horrible day at work. If I've said the wrong thing, you'll have to forgive me. I'm… not thinking straight.'

Marco dragged in some air. Everything he'd been working towards seemed to be falling apart, the balls he'd juggled dropping one by one. If she divorced him now, he would lose the estate and the dream he'd shared with Dario. If she was angry with him, disappointed that he'd let her down earlier, he might also lose his child.

'I'm doing all of this for my family,' he said, his voice pleading. 'Our baby will be a Caruso. He or she will inherit all of this one day. I have to finish things, honour my father…'

If she loved him, why was she leaving? Why was she taking his baby away without any plan to return?

She stood before him then, compassion in her eyes. 'You don't have to build so much as a sandcastle in order to honour your father, Marco. You can do it by being happy. By being the man you are—caring, honourable, a life-saver. You're just holding yourself back. You're scared to have any feelings in case you get hurt again, and I understand why because I felt the same.'

He frowned, his voice trapped in his throat as her words struck home like arrows.

Perhaps sensing he was at his limit, her expression softened, her voice dropping. 'I was scared of that too. Believe me, I understand the fear of letting a new person have a hold over your heart. But I don't want to live in fear any more, Marco. I want to love with my whole heart, but I also want to *be* loved the same way. Loved for the person I am and by the right man. One who cannot live without me, not one who only wants me in secret and to hang around in his guest house in order to ensure his inheritance.'

'So you're just leaving and taking a part of me, a part of this family with you?'

He should do something to make her stay, but he felt crushed by the weight of failure. The failure of their agreement, the failure of his dream to honour his father. And worse, the failure of his second marriage which, if he messed up, he might lose more than property this time. He might lose Elena and his child. For good.

'I'm leaving as we planned,' she said sadly, her voice resolved. 'That doesn't mean I'm breaking our arrangement. It will look like I've returned to Naples for work. We will divorce in a few months after you inherit. As for our baby, I will tell no one beyond my parents for the time being. We will discuss shared custody down the track. You are its father. I have no desire to hurt you or weaponise our child against you. I'm a Mancini, a woman you can never fully trust, but I am not out to ruin your plans. *I* trust you, Marco. I trust that we can be mature and respectful and put our baby first.'

'Of course we can… Elena…' He reached for her and she stepped back.

Outside, there came the toot of a horn.

'That's my taxi,' she said. 'I'm catching the last ferry to Naples.' She picked up her overnight bag.

'Let me carry that for you,' he said, desperate to delay what felt inevitable. If he could make her stay or make her return, he could analyse everything and come up with a solution.

'I've got it, thanks.' She headed for the door. 'Goodbye, Marco. I'll be in touch.'

And then, before he had time to even emerge from the shock of the multiple bombs she'd dropped, she left.

That night, Marco had barely slept. Every word of their arguments had replayed in his mind until his head had hurt and fire ants seemed to crawl over his skin. By four a.m. he had given up trying, arisen and headed for his home office to catch up on some work emails, only to be distracted by the mental image of Elena when she'd said *I love you*. By six a.m., unable to sit still a moment longer, he'd spent a solid hour running on the treadmill in the gym.

When even physical exhaustion had failed to take the edge off his internal trembling, he'd dived into the pool, hoping the cool water would shock him out of his bewilderment.

Now, after swimming fifty lengths, he paused to catch his breath. The oxygen seemed thin, the air poisoned. When a woman appeared at the top of the steps, his head spun with euphoria. It was Elena. His heart leapt, his body infused with adrenaline as if he could swim another fifty lengths with ease. But then his gut twisted with nausea as he recognised his sister.

'*Ciao*,' Gin called, giving him a wave.

Marco raised his hand, trying to smile through the pain in his chest. Gin rarely visited the estate since Dario's funeral. But she'd clearly chosen that day of all days to make an exception. A day when Marco wasn't sure how he would make it to nightfall, let alone how he would interact normally with other human beings.

He swam to the side of the pool and hauled himself from the water.

'I have papers for you to sign.' Gin waved a folder and then sat at the bistro table under the shade of an umbrella. Despite the early hour, the sun was already baking the terrace.

Marco wrapped a towel around his waist and joined his sister. After they embraced, Gin produced a fountain pen from her designer handbag.

'Here and here, please,' she said, flicking to the tabbed pages where his signature was required.

With another sharp stab to his chest, Marco recognised the document. It was the handover of the Caruso Enterprises shares of Dignità Hospice to Elena. His wedding gift.

With a trembling hand, Marco set the pen to the page just below Gin's own signature. But before he could sign, Gin placed her hand on his arm.

'You are sure about this?' She'd removed her sunglasses to reveal her concerned frown. 'You don't seem very happy about it.'

'*Sì.* I'm sure.' Marco added his signature where required and dropped the pen onto the table before turning away.

This was the one thing, the only thing he was certain about today. Where everything else in his life seemed to be built from sand. One rogue wave, one jolt and it would all come tumbling down.

'Is she here?' Gin asked, tucking the signed document back into its folder. 'Elena Mancini? I can hand this over personally. I'd like to meet this woman who has somehow managed to get under your skin.'

Marco ran his fingers through his slick hair, his legs weak from too much exercise. 'No. She left last night. For Naples.'

'Oh…' Gin frowned as if disappointed then looked up expectantly. 'Shall I leave it with you then?'

Marco swallowed, wondering how he would get the words out. 'No. She won't be back.' Even saying it aloud hurt. Elena had dropped not one but two bombshells and then left him alone to try to make sense of it all.

Of course, the minute he'd watched the taxi's rear lights disappear from view he'd felt a crushing weight of failure. The one thing he hadn't wanted to do was hurt his wife. But he'd somehow done that anyway.

'Why? What happened?' Gin pressed, her shrewd stare narrowing. 'I thought she was leaving today. That's why I made the early trip.'

'She…' Marco glanced out at the ocean and the mainland beyond as if he might see her and know she was okay. 'I…' He snatched a breath then sagged. 'It's over.'

His stomach rolled. He'd let her down. Accused her of leaking patient details to the press. Let her believe that he didn't trust her. Said the wrong things about the baby and let her leave.

'What's over?' Gin asked, coming to her feet. 'The ruse? The marriage?'

Marco shook his head, feeling dizzy, as if he couldn't breathe. 'No. She has promised to stay married to me until the estate is mine. But…'

'Marco…' Gin said carefully. 'You *were* sleeping with her, weren't you?' She gave a frustrated sigh. 'I told you to be careful. What happened?'

Marco swallowed, his silence confirmation

enough. 'Elena is pregnant,' he said, his heart leaping anew because this was the one piece of good news he could share. 'I'm going to be a father.'

Gin walked to him and wrapped her arms around his shoulders, clearly uncaring that he was still damp from the pool.

'Congratulations,' she said, holding his face, her smile the brave one she'd worn at their father's funeral.

'What?' he asked, feeling transparent, as if all his flaws and mistakes and regrets were on display for anyone to see. 'Why that look?'

She was seven years younger than him, but Gin had always seemed the more emotionally evolved.

'You're in love with her, aren't you?' she asked, although it was more of a statement. 'And somehow you've messed up, hurt her somehow, and let her leave you.' She dropped her hands from his face and crossed them over her waist, disappointed in him. 'Is she in love with you?'

Marco swallowed past a constricted throat and sank into a chair. 'She said she was. I want to support her and the baby, of course. But I warned her that there was no space in our arrangement for feelings. That I would not make another mistake. That I had an agenda I planned to stick to and—'

He broke off, his mind consumed with Elena and what he'd said and done and what he hadn't. He stood again, pacing, his body trying to outrun his thoughts and the terrible sense of doom he couldn't shake.

Gin shook her head, a pitying look on her face. 'It's not a mistake to love someone, Marco, especially not someone who loves you in return. Someone you are already married to, who is having your baby.' The look she gave him said *What's wrong with you?*

'I can't love her back, Gin. That's why she left.' He paced across the terrace to the edge of the pool. 'I have all these balls in the air and if I don't reach my goal, if I don't focus on the cancer centre and Papà's legacy, I'll have failed him again.'

When Gin stayed silent, he turned to see her resting her hands on her hips. 'You'll have failed Papà more if you are terminally alone and unhappy because you let this woman—one, by the way, it is glaringly obvious that you do love—go. You'll have failed him more if you lose your child, his grandchild, because you are stubbornly terrified of being vulnerable with another woman. We talk every week and I've seen a difference in you since this woman came into your life. I understand that you're scared to make another mistake, scared to lose something else. But she is not Bianca.'

'No,' he agreed, the depth of his devastation much deeper than when his first marriage had imploded. 'But that's why I'm trying to do the right thing,' he cried, gripping a handful of his hair. 'I can't lose anyone else. I can't lose my child. I can't lose El—'

He broke off, a fresh wave of nausea gripping his throat. He was scared to lose Elena so he'd done the one thing he'd vowed not to: pushed her away one final time. She'd opened her heart to him last night, bravely told him that despite him being a Caruso, despite the fact that their marriage wasn't real, she was in love with him.

And he, out of fear, had said nothing of his own feelings.

Marco slumped, his head in his hands as icy chills shivered through him, followed by wave after wave of devastating emotions. He loved Elena Mancini. He loved his wife. He loved her so much it had made him crazy. Blind. So overwhelmed he'd hurt her, said the wrong things and let her leave, believing that his inheritance and the cancer centre were more important to him than her and the baby. That the past was more important than his present and future—a place dominated by Elena.

Breathing hard, Marco braced his hands on his thighs.

'You do love her, don't you?' Gin said quietly, as if he might break.

Nauseated by the enormity of what he'd done, or failed to do, he nodded. Elena had challenged him from day one. Turned his tightly controlled and safe world upside down. Forced him to see himself more clearly than he ever had. To see that his coping mechanisms were only holding him back from the kind of happiness that was rare and ought to be clung to, not feared.

But was it too late? Could he change Elena's mind if he was finally honest with her? Could he persuade her to give him another chance? That he was finally ready to let go of the past, to forgive himself for his mistakes and build an emotionally healthier future. With her.

Then because he could not stand still a moment longer, he marched across the terrace, heading for the steps.

'Where are you going?' Gin asked.

'Naples,' he called, taking the steps two at a time. 'I should have told her she was right about me. About everything.'

'Take this.' Gin chased after him in her heels, brandishing the folder.

Marco paused halfway up, each second he waited for Gin to catch up agonising, as if he were living through the countdown to the end of the world. 'I have to go. I have to get her back.' He stared at his sister, silently pleading that she would help him out of the devastation he alone had created.

Gin nodded enthusiastically, holding out the documents then clinging when he tried to take it. 'Don't mess it up,' she said in warning. 'Tell her exactly how you feel.'

Marco swallowed and nodded. 'If I get the chance…'

The last thing he registered before he took off

running was his sister's worried frown, as if she too feared for him, feared that he'd left it too late to recognise his feelings.

CHAPTER SEVENTEEN

ELENA'S FAVOURITE PART of her Naples apartment in the hillside neighbourhood of Vomero had always been the small balcony. The views of the Bay of Naples and Mount Vesuvius were stunning. But as she sat there with her mother the morning after she'd left Marco, she couldn't bear to glance that way towards Capri. Because Marco was there and he couldn't love her back.

'He seemed a little stronger this morning,' Amara Mancini said about Gio, whom they had visited that morning.

'Yes. He was in good spirits.' Elena dragged in a deep breath. 'Mamma, I have things to tell you.'

'Okay,' her mother said, taking a sip of *limonata*.

'I'm having a baby,' Elena said. 'It's due in the spring.'

Amara's face lit up. She leaned close and embraced her daughter. 'Oh, I am so pleased! Congratulations! Papà will be overjoyed! Why didn't you tell us both this morning?'

Elena glanced down at her lap. 'It's...complicated. I wanted to tell you first. Then you can decide how much we should tell Papà,' Elena said, fanning her T-shirt against the heat.

Amara reached for her hand. '*Cara*, you are worrying me. What is it? Is there something wrong?'

Elena shook her head, although everything was wrong. She was in love with a man she'd promised to divorce. A man whose baby she was having, one who couldn't love her back. And her parents didn't even know about her arrangement with Marco.

'Well, the thing is…' she said, looking up, her face growing hot, 'the baby's father is Marco Caruso.'

Amara frowned. 'Dario's son? The surgeon?'

Elena nodded. 'I know. I should have told you sooner, but, well… I ended up working for him in Capri and we kind of began a relationship. But now it's over.'

Amara patted the back of Elena's hand. 'I'm sorry to hear that.'

Elena nodded and blinked, her eyes filling with tears. 'I know it's hard to understand. Working for him felt very disloyal at first. But then I got to know him, to see what a dedicated surgeon he is. Then I found out that Dario died not long after Medicina dell'Apparenza closed.'

Amara gasped, her hand covering her mouth. 'I didn't know that.'

Elena shook her head. 'Me neither. I haven't mentioned I was working with him all these weeks because I don't want to upset Papà by reminding him of the past.'

Amara tsked. 'It is not your burden to carry,

Elena. I know how loyal you are, but Gio made his peace with what happened a long time ago. Realising your own mortality will do that to a person. That's why you have to find happiness and live every day of your life to the fullest. Because we all have to make our own choices, and none of us know what is around the corner.'

Elena nodded as her eyes filled with tears, glancing away from her mother's perceptive stare. 'There's more,' she said, swallowing hard. This would be the most difficult part to confess. 'I actually married him. Marco, I mean.'

Amara's eyes rounded and Elena rushed on. 'It was supposed to be temporary so he could inherit the Caruso estate, and I would get Papà's hospice for the Mancini Foundation. We are supposed to divorce in a few months.'

'Are you in love with him?' Amara asked, her shrewd eyes no doubt seeing everything.

'Yes,' Elena said, sniffing bravely. 'But he won't let me in. He can't love me back. He's too hung up on the past and making amends to his father to recognise that what we have could be special. So I have to accept that it's over. That by loving him I made another mistake. I have to move on now and focus on the baby.'

'Love is never a mistake, *cara*,' her mother said. 'It's okay to be hurt when someone lets you down. But don't regret that you put your whole heart into something, into someone you thought was worthy.

Don't diminish yourself and your beautiful feelings just because they aren't reciprocated.'

Elena shook her head, wiping at the tears that spilled onto her cheeks. 'No, you are right. I can hold my head up and know that I made my child out of love. I know Marco will be a good father and that will be enough.'

'Are you sure?' Amara asked with a frown. 'I will always support you and your decisions. But don't let what happened with Rocco harden your heart too much. Remember that love makes us brave.'

Elena swallowed, part of her desperate to be strong for the baby and her own peace of mind. But had she run away too quickly, still scared to fully believe in love? A part of her would always love Marco. There was no shame in that. Maybe it was time to forgive herself for her past mistakes and admit all of her feelings to Marco, even if he could not love her back.

Every minute of the fifty-five-minute ferry journey from Capri to Naples had felt like a year. Marco had found Elena's address from her CV and as the taxi pulled up outside her building he flung open the door, handing the driver a wad of euros that would most likely cover the fare three times over. Not that he cared.

At the door to her building, he pressed the buzzer for Elena's apartment, his feet shuffling on the stone step. He was just about to press it a second time when the outer door opened and an elegant woman in her fifties appeared.

She took one look at him and gasped. 'Marco Caruso,' she said, her eyes wide with shock and a hint of accusation that was less than he deserved.

He recognised her too. This was Elena's mother.

'Signora Mancini,' he said, reaching for her hand. 'Pleased to meet you. Forgive me… I wish we could have met under better circumstances. I wish I had time to meet you properly now, introduce myself properly.' His words tumbled out. 'But I love your daughter, and I need to tell her immediately. Beg her to give me another chance. I'm sorry.'

'Then you had better hurry.' Signora Mancini stepped aside and held open the door for him to enter the building.

With his pulse pounding and his head light from lack of oxygen, Marco squeezed the woman's hand. 'Thank you. Pray for me, *signora*.'

He was just about to bound up the stairs when he stopped and turned. 'I know I have no right, but I have one more request. I plan to propose to your daughter, if she will forgive me. I know how much family means to her, means to us both, so I ask that you and Signore Mancini consider giving me your blessing.'

Amara Mancini looked him over from head to toe, her hesitation agonising because every second kept him from Elena. 'If my daughter deems you worthy of her hand, then neither of you need our blessing,' she said. 'You will understand when your own child is born that, as parents, all we want is for our children to be happy. Only Elena knows if you are the man for that job.'

'*Grazie mille*.' Resting one hand on her shoulder, Marco kissed both her cheeks. 'I will spend the rest of my life with that very goal, if she will have me.'

'Then go,' she said, her hazel eyes, so much like her daughter's, shining. 'Don't waste another precious second, young man.'

And with those words ringing in his head, Marco bounded up the stairs, taking them two at a time.

CHAPTER EIGHTEEN

'WHAT DID YOU FORGET, MAMMA?' Elena said, flinging open the door to her apartment. But rather than her mother on the doorstep, it was Marco. 'What are you doing here?' Her heart clenched painfully at the handsome sight of him. But he was breathless, his hair dishevelled and his eyes tired as if, like her, he had slept poorly.

'Elena, please,' he begged. 'Let me in. I need to talk to you, to apologise, to tell you things… Please…'

Elena stepped aside to allow him entrance, careful to keep her body away from his, to keep her defences up. Even an accidental touch would weaken her resolve. The very fact that he was there trapped the air in her chest and left her light-headed with euphoric hope that he might have changed his mind and want a real relationship. Then she noticed the folder clutched in his hand.

'What's that?' she asked, eyeing it warily as she felt the blood drain from her face. Had he changed his mind and already instigated divorce proceedings? Was he there for her signature to dissolve the marriage?

He glanced down at his hand as if he'd forgotten he was holding something. 'Oh, it's the transfer documentation for Dignità. It came through this morning and I wanted you to have it.'

Elena took the folder he held out, her hand trembling, and placed it on a nearby console table. 'Thank you. You could have e-mailed it. No need to deliver it personally.'

She stepped away from him, the contents of the folder another knife through her heart. Clearly, for Marco, their arrangement was still very much intact and still his number one priority.

'I had to come,' he said, following her into the room. 'I—' His voice broke and Elena took a closer look at him.

There were dark shadows around his eyes. His rumpled clothes appeared hastily chosen and thrown on and there was a twitchy, agitated quality to his movements that made her wonder if he'd drunk too much coffee.

'I have to apologise, Elena,' he said, gripping a handful of his hair.

'What for?' she asked, fighting her natural instinct to comfort him somehow. He looked…broken.

'For it all,' he said, flinging out an arm. 'For the way I treated you when we first met. For the resentment I carried against your father and your family. For coercing you into an appalling marriage in name only. Forgive me.'

'You did not coerce me,' Elena said stiffly because while nice to hear, his declarations weren't what she craved. 'I willingly agreed. And our arrangement worked.' She gestured to the folder he'd brought. 'We will both finally have everything we wanted.'

'No.' He vigorously shook his head and took another step closer. 'I don't care about the past or my inheritance or even the Caruso Cancer Centre. I just want you.'

Elena shook her head, shutting down the dangerous flare of hope that sparked inside her chest. 'You mean you want our child. Your heir. Another Caruso you can leave the estate to. I told you I would not interfere with your relationship with our baby. If you trusted me, you would know that.'

'No,' he replied with more force, his stare so intent, his face so haggard she had to cross her arms to stop herself from reaching for him. 'I want *you*. If there was no baby, I'd still be standing here begging you to forgive me and give me another chance. And I do trust you. I know you the way you know me. I know your joy and your compassion and your loyalty.'

Elena swallowed, her entire body now trembling as she hovered close to wavering. She could end the doubt and devastation of the past twenty-four hours with just one touch, one kiss. But the joy would be short-lived. She couldn't take him back if he could never love her.

Shaking her head, she glanced down. 'I can't, Marco. I want more than a convenient relationship built on a lie.' She looked up and saw only panic in his eyes. 'I want all of you, not just your home and financial protection. I don't even need the thing that started all of this, the hospice. I just need you. To love me as desperately as I love you. Because I've forgiven myself for the mistake I made in the past in trusting my ex. I want to be emotionally healthy and love with my whole heart. To have the life I deserve. Love, marriage, a family and career. I want it all.'

'And you have all of me, Elena,' he said, closing the distance between them and resting one hand over his heart. 'I love you. Exactly the same way. I think I fell in love with you that first week when you called me a robot. That's why I'm here. To tell you that nothing matters to me more than *you.* More than what we could have together if, rather than divorcing, we both put our all into this marriage and made it real.'

Elena blinked, her eyes stinging harder with his every word. Her pulse buzzed. Could she believe him? Could she trust that he was sincere? That he'd forgiven himself too?

As if sensing her doubts, Marco reached for both of her hands. 'You were right about me, Elena. I've been stuck grieving, fooling myself that if I kept my promise to my father, the pain of my failures would disappear. But I'm not a robot. I'm a man. I'm flawed and broken and sometimes arrogant. But losing you finally put things into sharp perspective, helped me to see what I really want. What I truly need to be happy. And it's not the estate or the cancer centre or even an heir, although I want to raise our baby with you. It's love. *Your* love. I love you and I'll spend the rest of my life proving it to you, showing you with actions not words. Just please give me a chance.'

'Marco…' she whispered, raising her left hand to cup his unshaven face, softly gasping when she saw the truth behind every one of his words in his eyes.

His expression twisted with agony as he covered her hand with his, holding it to his face then kissing the centre of her palm.

'I love you,' he croaked, his voice thick with emotion. 'For the wonderful, caring, loving woman that you are. Because of who you are, Elena Mancini. Because you've helped me to forgive myself. I'll never let you down again, I swear. I'll do anything—anything to win you back.'

'Then kiss me,' she said, her entire body tingling as she smiled at the man she loved.

With an anguished groan, his expression sagging with relief, he pulled her into his arms. His lips covered hers and heat surged through her as she collapsed against his hard chest and wrapped her arms around him. His heart was a rapid thud against hers as their kisses deepened, their tongues surging together, their moans mingling.

Then he pulled back. 'Forgive me,' he begged, one hand cupping her face.

'There's nothing to forgive,' she cried. 'I could

have trusted my instincts more and given you time to figure out your feelings. I just… I was scared to trust what I felt, scared that I'd made another mistake. But I'm no longer scared. I trust this. I believe in us.'

Marco pressed his lips to her forehead. 'I was a fool. So hung up on the past that I missed what was right in front of me. You. Love. I thought I had everything under control. And then I met you and nothing has been the same since.'

'In a good way?' she asked, pulling back to give him a challenging look while her lips twitched.

'In the best way.' He smiled and her breath caught. 'You were right, Elena. About everything. My father would want me to be happy above all else. And I've no hope of that unless it's with you.'

Elena smiled wider, her heart fluttering with joy. 'You do realise that there might be one or two family members who think we're crazy?' she said, running her fingers through his windswept hair. 'A Caruso and a Mancini…'

'I'm crazy about my wife,' he said, holding her tighter, and she laughed. 'That's all that counts. The rest was never our fight, *cara*.'

'No,' she said softly. 'Time to leave the past behind and look forward to the future. Our future.'

Marco cupped her face, his stare searching hers. 'About the baby… I'm overjoyed. Ecstatic. Last night I was in shock, but I can't wait to be a father. I can't wait to love you as the mother to our child.

Will you…come back to Capri? When you're ready. So we can figure everything out.'

Elena's eyes stung with happy tears. 'Of course. I love you. I'll always want to be where you are. Although I have another locum position here in Naples for the next three weeks.'

He wrapped his arms around her and held her tight. 'Come to me at the weekends. Or I will come here.'

Elena nodded and kissed him, her heart bursting with love.

'I will always love you, *cara*,' he said when they broke apart.

'Then love me now,' she said, unbuttoning his shirt.

So he did.

Marco lay in Elena's bed as afternoon morphed into evening, the sun outside setting behind Mount Vesuvius. Her naked body was draped over his, their legs tangled and her arms wrapped around him as if she'd never let him go. His skin was coated in the scent of her perfume, strands of her hair caught in his beard and he never wanted to move from this spot.

He slid his fingers through that thick, luxuriant hair, gently untangling snags. But sleepy and satisfied, dishevelled and flushed from pleasure, she'd never looked more perfect or beautiful. Or his.

Raising her left hand to his lips, he kissed her

bare ring finger, that possessive swell washing over him now that he'd earned a second chance to make her properly his. 'You've taken off your wedding ring,' he said idly, realising how used he'd grown to seeing the gold band on her finger. Oh, how he wished he'd stopped to buy her a diamond to go alongside it. But he'd been too desperate to win her back to stop. For anything, even that.

She raised her head from his chest. 'I went to visit my father this morning,' she said. 'I've been taking it off every weekend. I wasn't ready to explain what I'd done. Can you imagine me trying to explain that? A fake marriage to a Caruso…'

Marco smiled, but then frowned. 'How is he doing, *cara*?' he asked, sliding his fingers between hers as their hearts beat side by side.

'He's the same,' she said, her beautiful eyes dulling with sadness. 'Good days and bad. I've told my mother about the marriage and the baby. I'm leaving it up to her how much she shares with Papà.'

'I know.' Marco nodded, his love for his incredible wife almost suffocating. 'I met your mother on the doorstep downstairs.'

'You did?' Elena sat up, her mouth agape. 'What did she say to you?'

Marco cupped her cheek, brushing the pad of his thumb over her lips because he wanted to kiss her again. 'She said she wants you to be happy and that we do not need her or your father's blessing.'

'Blessing for what?' Elena frowned. 'It's a bit

late for that. We're already legally married, and I'm having your baby.'

'For this.' Marco pressed a soft kiss to her lips then slid from the bed, getting down on one knee and reaching for her hand.

'Marco…' she whispered, eyes nervous but smiling. 'You're naked and on your knees…'

'I've been on my knees since the day we met,' he said, pressing a kiss to the back of her hand. He looked up. 'Elena, *cara*, I thought I was done with love when I met you, but love was not done with me. I tried to fight my feelings for you, and that fight almost broke me. I don't want a divorce, ever. In fact, I want to marry you again, properly this time. For all the right reasons and with all our loved ones present. No pre-nup. No conditions. And not for appearances' sake.'

'Marco,' she whispered, her beautiful eyes shining with tears.

'Everything I have is yours, *cara*. Everything that I am is also yours if you will have me. Because I am only half a man without you. So, Elena Gia Mancini, I don't yet have an engagement ring, but will you marry me again? For real this time.'

She laughed and smiled and nodded, tugging his hands to bring his mouth to hers. 'Yes, I will.' She kissed him again and Marco's breath caught in his chest with relief.

He pulled back and she chased him, peppering kisses over his face. 'I promise that for the rest of our lives, I will show you that I love you. They are not just words.'

'Marco,' she said on sigh and she urged him back to bed and pulled him down on top of her. 'I love you so much. Show me now.'

He kissed her slowly, lazily, her love finally filling the void inside him so he knew with all certainty that they would face any challenges in their future together, side by side. And because he was a perfectionist, because he never again intended to let her down or disappoint her, he set about loving his wife the way she deserved.

EPILOGUE

One year later

THE CARUSO ESTATE glittered and gleamed in the sunshine of another stunning Mediterranean day. Elena stood facing Marco under a bougainvillea-draped gazebo to renew her vows before the very celebrant who had married them the first time around, something Marco had arranged as a surprise.

She held his hands, lost in his loving gaze, her breath catching at the sheer romance of their second wedding ceremony.

'These rings,' the female celebrant said, 'are a symbol of the loving, committed statements you have made to one another, here today in front of your guests.'

Elena smiled at her handsome husband and glanced around those congregated to help them celebrate. This time, their wedding was a true family affair. Dino was Marco's best man and Marco's sister, Gin, stood as Elena's maid of honour. Enzo had walked Elena down the aisle in place of Gio, who had sadly lost his battle with Parkinson's four months after she'd moved back to Capri. The birth of her and Marco's son at the very hospital where they'd met had gone a long way towards helping everyone through the grieving process. Baby Gio sat now with both his *nonnas* and his honorary *nonna*, Maria. And behind them, with his wife at his side, sat Fredo Degano, the patient who had brought her and Marco together, cancer-free after his chemotherapy.

Taking Marco's ring, Elena slid it onto his finger, smiling up at him with so much love she felt faint with happiness. 'My ring is a symbol of my endless love, wrapped around you for ever.'

He was a wonderful husband—loving, protective, passionate—and a doting father. He shown her over and over again that he would always support her dreams, suggesting that if she wanted to finish her surgical training they relocate to Naples or Rome as a family.

Marco swallowed, clearly choked by her words. Then he did the same, slowly gliding the gold band into place on her ring finger, his eyes ablaze with love and a thrilling possessive heat that spoke louder than any vow. 'My ring is yours, just as my heart is yours and will be for ever.'

Elena blinked up at him, smiling. His dreams were hers and vice versa. Marco still planned to finish the Caruso Cancer Centre, but it was no longer his only goal or his reason to be happy. That they had found together, in their love for each other.

'Elená and Marco,' the registrar continued with a broad smile, 'after once more committing yourselves to each other and to your union, I now pronounce you are still lawfully joined in matrimony. I wish you a long and happy marriage and good luck. Congratulations!'

As the guests clapped and cheered, Marco drew Elena into his arms, holding her against his chest as he gazed down at her, his eyes dipping to her lips. '*Amore mio*,' he said, one hand cupping her cheek as if he couldn't quite believe she was real, 'I love you and I want you to know that this has absolutely nothing to do with appearances.'

Then he kissed her, slowly and thoroughly, his hands holding her face, his lips parting and his tongue sliding against hers as he groaned a sexy sound in the back of his throat. Elena kissed him back as if they were alone, uncaring that their passion for each other was on display. But when they pulled back, grinning at each other, laughing joyously, she dragged in a shaky breath.

'Keep it PG in front of the baby, Signore Caruso,' she teased, laughing up at him.

Marco's joy rumbled in his chest as he pressed his lips to her forehead. 'Only until he's asleep tonight,' he whispered for her ears only. 'Then I'm afraid all deals are off, Signora Caruso.'

With his adult promise driving her pulse to dizzying heights, Marco turned to accept his baby son from Nonna Mancini. Cradling the baby in one arm, he kept the other arm around Elena. She watched in wonder as he pressed a tender kiss to baby Gio's head and whispered words of affection that tugged at Elena's already bursting heart.

And as all three of them mingled with their friends and family, accepting congratulations and hugs and well-wishes, Elena sighed happily, knowing that their love, their heartfelt vows to each other and even the pleasure Marco promised once they were alone, was an arrangement she could live with for the rest of her life.

* * * * *

If you enjoyed this story, check out these other great reads from JC Harroway

Doctor Boss with Benefits
The Paramedic Roommate Pact
Mistletoe Baby Mix-Up
One Night to Royal Baby

All available now!